KEEPING HAPPILY EVER AFTER

ELENA AITKEN

Keeping Happily Ever After

Also by Elena Aitken

Ever After

The Springs Series

His to Tame

His to Seek

Hers for the Season

Bears of Grizzly Ridge: Books 1-4

Bears of Grizzly Ridge: Books 5-8

Halfway Series

Halfway to Nowhere

Halfway in Between

Halfway to Christmas

Chapter One

IT WAS COLD. Really cold. The type of cold that froze your eyelashes to your face the moment you set foot outside. February in the mountains was no joke. Which was exactly why a rookie should have been the one heading to the grocery store in the deep freeze, instead of Jeremy Davis. But when the fire chief gave you an order, you didn't pass it off. Even to a rookie. Even when it was absolutely ridiculous that Jeremy had to be the one to go to the grocery store that afternoon to pick up fresh rosemary, of all things.

The saving grace in the entire situation was that Ed Walker, the fire chief, was an amazing cook and if he wanted fresh rosemary, it meant there was going to be pot roast on the menu that night. Jeremy's mouth watered at the thought. Most of the firefighters had become good cooks over the years out of necessity, but Ed was by far the best. Likely because he'd been at it the longest, which was also why the rumors were only heating up that Ed was getting ready to retire and appoint a new chief. A role that Jeremy had been working toward since he'd joined the Glacier Falls fire department seven years ago as a rookie himself.

In a small mountain town like Glacier Falls, the department hadn't been very big even when Jeremy had joined. But over the last few years, they'd grown, along with the town, and even though at only twenty-seven, Jeremy might still be considered a rookie, he was ready for the challenge of a growing fire department.

"But first," he muttered to himself as he steered the department pickup truck down the icy street, "rosemary."

He was just about to take the turn in to the grocery store lot when his radio crackled to life.

"Davis, possible sparks detected over at Burton's place," the voice said.

Shit.

He was only half a block away. Even without the rig, he was the logical dispatch. "10-4," he said quickly into the radio. "On my way."

Jeremy flicked his light on, shoulder checked and quickly changed course.

He'd been hoping there wouldn't be another call out to Roy Burton's place before they managed to move the elderly man into the retirement home he'd finally agreed to. Especially because Jeremy knew he was in the house alone. Before Christmas, the fire department had responded regularly to calls at Roy's house. Thankfully, that had changed after Bella, Roy's granddaughter, came to town for the holidays and convinced him it was time to move.

But Bella, Jeremy knew, wasn't with her grandfather at the moment. She'd returned to the city in the middle of January, and now, two weeks later she still wasn't due back for two days, ten hours, and four more minutes.

Not that he was counting.

And although it would be safer for Roy to have Bella back in town, Jeremy also was selfishly concerned with himself and how great it would be to have her back in his arms once again.

2

And his bed.

He shook his head to clear it as he pulled up in front of Roy's house. He would allow himself to think about Bella later. First things first: making sure Roy was okay and hadn't set his kitchen on fire. Again.

He moved quickly, grabbing a fire extinguisher from the backseat before running up the steps and banging on the door. "Roy?" He knocked again. "Roy, you in there?"

Without waiting for an answer, Jeremy tried the door handle. And just as it always did, the door opened freely. He stepped across the threshold and called out again. "Roy?"

Jeremy sniffed the air for smoke. Nothing.

He scanned the room. Nothing seemed out of place.

And then a flicker of movement caught his eye. He turned and subsequently froze as his brain registered what he was seeing.

"Bella?"

The most beautiful woman he'd ever seen leaned against the doorframe that led to the kitchen. Her long, dark, wavy hair cascaded over her bare shoulder. Jeremy let out a low whistle as he took in the sight of the woman he was very rapidly falling in love with, wearing nothing more than a red silky negligee and a wicked smile on her face.

But he needed to focus.

"Roy? Is he—"

"Fine." Bella stepped toward him. "Safely next door with Lydia."

Jeremy's brain was having trouble keeping up. "So there are no sparks?" As he said it out loud, he realized it was a ridiculous call. Never in his career had he ever been called out for *possible sparks.*

Now, only inches away, Bella reached out for the collar of his jacket and pulled him toward her as she shook her head.

"Not yet," she whispered against his mouth. "But hopefully soon there'll be a few."

It wasn't until she pressed her sensuous lips to his and kissed him fully that Jeremy allowed himself to believe what he was seeing was real. *Bella. In his arms.* Earlier than two days, ten hours, and four more minutes.

He broke the kiss long enough to set the fire extinguisher down, and scoop Bella up so he could carry her down the hall into her bedroom.

"Tell me again." Jeremy shook his head and laughed. "How did you make this happen?"

It had been less than two weeks since Bella had left Glacier Falls for the city. Barely enough time to take care of the meetings she had scheduled with her new agent and casting directors that her new friend, the mega celebrity Stephanie Starz, had introduced her to after hearing Bella sing at Christmas on her last visit to Glacier Falls. *More than one awesome thing had happened on that trip*, she thought as she let her eyes travel up Jeremy's hard, naked chest.

Umm. It was good to be back in his arms. *Very* good. As much fun as she'd had in the city, what she'd just done with Jeremy—and hoped to do again very soon—was pretty damn fun, too.

There had been a few very exciting weeks as she sang for more people than she could remember and even ran lines for potential movie roles, something she'd never considered doing. But even though she'd been so busy she barely had time to sleep, she still had a lot of time to miss Jeremy terribly. Which was why she'd decided to return to town earlier than planned. Definitely a good decision, judging by the smile on Jeremy's face as he laid on his side, propped up on a pillow with the bed sheet slipping just a little off his bare hip. She let her fingers trace along his smooth skin where the sheet rested and he shivered under her touch. *Yes.* She'd definitely made the right decision to come back early.

"I knew you had to work," Bella explained for the third time. "So I called in a favor with the chief. He's still pretty pleased with me for singing at the Christmas Eve dinner." She grinned and then squealed as Jeremy reached out and, in a move so quick, she didn't have time to react, pulled her on top of him.

Her squeals quickly dissolved into satisfied moans as he wrapped his arms around her and kissed her deeply again. They'd just finished making love and reacquainting themselves with each other, but that didn't seem to matter to Jeremy. Or her. Except for the fact that she'd promised her grandfather they'd start packing later that afternoon, the only thing she had to do was lie there with him and enjoy each other completely.

Reluctantly, Bella pushed herself up from his chest. "We can't," she protested. "Not again. We don't have time. My grandfather will be home anytime. And I promised I'd help him pack up."

"One more kiss. And then I want to hear all about your meetings and how famous you're going to be." He pulled her back down onto him, and she couldn't bring herself to protest as his hands slid up her bare back.

In fact, ten minutes later, she still wasn't protesting, but was participating fully in his distraction techniques when they both heard the front door open.

"Shit." Jeremy jumped up like a teenager caught by his girlfriend's parents and grabbed a pillow to cover his naked body with.

Bella couldn't help it; she burst out laughing and only belatedly slapped a hand over her mouth to stifle her giggles. A technique that didn't work very well as the laughter slipped out between her fingers when Jeremy started dashing around the room, looking for his clothes.

"Bella! This isn't funny."

"It is, though." She tried to swallow her laughter, but failed. "It really is." She probably could have laughed at him all afternoon, but the genuine horror on his face when he couldn't find his pants spurred her into action. "Okay, fine."

It's not as if they were going to go back to fooling around, anyway. She might as well help him out.

It only took Bella a few seconds to gather his clothes. She pulled his pants from the twisted quilt at the foot of the bed, and tossed them in his direction. "Honestly, Jeremy. It's okay. He gets it. He does." But even as she said the words, she didn't believe them. Not really. It was one thing for her grandfather to know about them dating, and another for him to see it in graphic detail.

Obviously, Jeremy agreed and quickly pulled his pants on before tugging his sweater into place. "Easy for you to say. You're his sweet, perfect granddaughter who can do no wrong. I'm just the guy sleeping with her."

His choice of words stopped her and she turned to look at him halfway through tugging her leggings on. "That's it? You're just the guy *sleeping* with me?" She didn't want it to, but his nonchalance bothered her. More than she thought it might. After all, they had only been together since Christmas. Less than a month. They weren't serious. The words girlfriend and boyfriend were barely even used. In fact, they hadn't really discussed anything serious about their relationship or their future and—

"No." He interrupted her train of thought. Thankfully before her thoughts could spiral too far in a negative direction. Jeremy stood in front of her and grabbed her hands, forcing her to focus on him. "That is definitely not all I am, babe. I am *so* much more than that. At least I want to be. You know that."

She nodded and her smile was genuine. "I do."

"Good." Jeremy leaned in to kiss her. "In fact…I would really like to be—"

"Bella?"

Jeremy jumped at the sound of her grandfather's bellow, causing Bella to laugh again.

"One minute, Papa. I'll be right there."

She quickly finished getting dressed. "Can we finish this conversation later?"

"That's a promise." He kissed her again, and Bella melted into it the way she always did.

She forced herself to pull away from him again. Something that was becoming harder and harder to do. "Come on. Let's go say hi." Bella took his hand and led him out to the living room. She'd only been back with Jeremy for a few hours, and already the idea of being away from him again was becoming impossible to fathom.

And that was a problem. A big problem. Because those meetings she'd had in the city had been very promising. And if everything went according to plan, and the way she hoped, she was going to be spending a lot more time in the city and away from him.

Bella snuck a glance at Jeremy as he greeted her grandfather with a hug.

Or, she was going to have a very big decision to make.

Either way, she wasn't looking forward to it.

The last thing Bella wanted to do after kissing Jeremy one final good-bye on the porch was help her grandfather pack up the house he'd lived in for decades. What she really wanted to do was have a long, hot bath, and curl up in her bed with a good book. Not that she'd even be able to get through a full chapter before falling asleep. She was exhausted, with a type of tired she hadn't felt in a very long time. The type that permeated through every single cell of her body. But it wasn't just her muscles that were tired—it was her brain.

The last few weeks had been a whirlwind of meetings, auditions, and sound tests of all kinds. Not that she was complaining. Not at all. All of her dreams were finally coming true, in a huge way. It had only taken a few good words from Stephanie Starz, who not only happened to be the biggest star in all of Hollywood, but was also a new friend, and before Bella knew it, she had a talent agent and more meetings and interviews and auditions in a one-week period than she'd had in her entire career up until then. Never mind the opportunities that had opened up. She'd gone from auditioning for small gigs in smokey basement bars, to having actual auditions and sound checks for major Hollywood casting agents. Her head still spun with how quickly things had changed.

In the living room, Bella stretched her arms over her head as she inhaled a deep breath and filled her lungs. She held the pose for a moment before exhaling slowly and dropping her arms and folding her body in half.

"What on earth are you doing?"

Her grandfather's voice startled her into breaking the posture.

Bella stood and smiled in his direction before folding over again. "Yoga, Papa. It helps me relax."

Papa made a snorting noise and Bella stifled a giggle. He was so old school, no doubt he still thought yoga was some sort of new age—

"I never understood that new age hippy bullshit."

She didn't even try to hide her laughter this time. Bella burst out laughing and stood tall. With a shake of her head, she moved to kiss her grandfather on the cheek. "You are nothing if not predictable, Papa."

He frowned and shook his head. "I'm just saying—"

"It's okay." Bella moved across the living room. "I love you just the way you are." And she did. She'd spent far too long away from him and the small town of Glacier Falls, where she used to spend her time as a child. It wasn't since returning at Christmas that she realized just how much she'd missed it. Of course, reconnecting with Jeremy, who'd been her childhood crush and first kiss, had definitely helped her favorable feelings toward the small mountain town.

Her face heated, at the thought of Jeremy and the way she'd surprised him a few hours earlier. *His hands on her skin, his lips on hers. The way his arms caged her in as he—*

"Bella?"

She spun around at the touch of her grandfather's hand on her shoulder and let out a small squeak of surprise before catching herself. She really did need to get some rest if she planned to focus on anything at all.

"Sorry, Papa. I was just thinking about—"

"Oh, I know." He interrupted her. "You have more important things on your mind than helping an old man." He didn't sound upset in any way, but Bella couldn't help but feel guilty. "I really do appreciate you being here, baby girl. Especially because I know you have your own life to live and it's an exciting one, to be sure. If you need to take care of business, you go right ahead, Bella. I don't want to keep you from anything."

"Papa?" She moved a little so she stood directly in front of her grandfather. He'd always been such a big man. Every summer when she came to spend a few months with him, she remembered thinking that he was the biggest, toughest man she knew. Even though year after year, she got taller and caught up with him a little bit more, he remained a larger-than-life figure in her world. Now in his eighties, he no longer had the strength she remembered, and he'd lost a little of his height, but he still had the same presence of the man who made her feel safe and loved as a child. "There is no place I'd rather be," she said slowly. "Don't think for a moment that you are inconveniencing me in any way. I'm just a little tired, but I promise you have my full attention."

His lips twitched up a little in a smile. "If you're sure."

"I'm sure."

"Okay," he said slowly. "Because Lydia mentioned she could give me a hand as well, so if you're ever too busy, or…"

"Oh?" Bella wiggled her eyebrows. "I see what's happening here. You're trying to get rid of me so I don't cramp your style with the lady next door." She shook her head with a laugh and grabbed a box.

"I didn't say that."

She turned and gave him a wink over her shoulder. "You didn't have to."

Chapter Two

JEREMY COULD HAVE HAPPILY SPENT the rest of the day in Bella's bed. Or thinking about Bella. Or dreaming of Bella and the way her mouth made that perfect circle and her eyes squeezed tight when she was climaxing. Oh yes, he could have very happily spent the rest of the day thinking about that moment, or better yet, reliving it. Unfortunately, despite the extended break his chief, Ed Walker, had afforded him, his shift was far from over.

It would only be the memory of Bella in that red negligee, her dark hair falling over her shoulder as she leaned against the doorframe that would be keeping him warm through the rest of the cold February night, because his shift didn't end until morning. Not that he minded working. Not at all. He loved his job. Serving as a firefighter for his hometown had long been a dream of Jeremy's. There was literally nothing else he could imagine himself doing for a living.

But that didn't mean he couldn't imagine himself in a whole lot of different positions at that very moment with one very sexy, petite brunette.

With a deeply unsatisfied groan—because he knew that was exactly what he *wouldn't* be doing that night—Jeremy pushed up from the easy chair in the station lounge and moved to the restroom, where he let the water run cold.

"Focus, Davis."

He splashed and scrubbed the icy-cold water over his face and looked up into the mirror at his reflection. There was a permanent grin in place. It had been there since Christmas Eve when Bella returned to town, surprising him and affirming that she, too, felt that there was something developing between them. Something that could be...love? Jeremy chuckled at himself and shook his head. It wasn't a question. It had never been a question. He was very much falling in love with Bella Burton. Maybe a part of him always had been.

She'd been his first kiss when they were kids and maybe it was that early experience. Or maybe it was just that Bella was beautiful and talented and kind and generous and the most perfect woman he'd ever met. But whatever it was, Jeremy knew in his heart that she was the one for him. It might still be early days in their relationship. *Very* early days. Hell, they hadn't even made it official by putting a label on it, or whatever it was they were supposed to do, but it didn't matter. Not to him. He'd do his best to be patient with things, especially because Bella's career was just starting to take off. But he knew what he wanted, and it was Bella.

"Davis?" A sharp knock on the door jarred him from his daydreams of Bella. "You in there?" His rookie partner, Natalie Collins, shouted through the door.

He grabbed a towel and dried his face. "Yup. Just finishing up."

"Your dad's here. Waiting in the lounge."

Dad?

It wasn't totally unusual for his father to pop by the station to say hi, but it was starting to get late. He should be home with his mother, getting ready for dinner, not stopping by for social visits.

"Hey, Dad." Dwayne Davis had his back to Jeremy when he walked into the room. He was looking out the window to the street below. Jeremy knew before he even turned around that something was wrong. His normally relaxed, easygoing father looked tense. He held himself straight, as if he were trying to shoulder the weight of the world. "What's up?" Jeremy resisted the urge to ask him what was wrong.

Sure enough, as soon as he turned around, Jeremy could see it. The worry lines ran deep in the older man's forehead. His normally smiling, happy face was twisted into a mask of worry. "Sorry to bother you at work like this, son. I was just... well, it just couldn't..."

"Dad?" Jeremy crossed the room in two big strides. He put his arm around his father's shoulder and guided him to the couch. "What's going on? Is it Mom? Is everything—"

"She's fine." Dwayne sat heavily next to his son. "Your mother is fine. We're both fine. It's not that. I'm sorry, Jer. I didn't mean to worry you, and I was hoping this could wait for a better time, or at least until I knew something definitely." He looked away, staring into nothing for a moment. "I was really hoping I wouldn't have to say anything at all and that I was wrong. But sometimes when you know, you just know, and I knew the moment I—"

"Dad." Jeremy put his hand on his father's forearm and forced Dwayne to look at him. "Tell me what the hell is going on."

Dwayne was known for being down to earth and excessively calm. Jeremy could recall very few occasions he'd ever seen him worked up. Even when there was a real estate deal with multiple offers, or at risk of being lost entirely when he was working with Jeremy's mother as the town's top real estate agents. Triple D Realty. Dwayne and Darlene Davis. They'd worked hard, but always together. And even when times were tough, they managed to have fun together. Jeremy had definitely never seen this type of worry on his father's face before. Not even during the recession when the real estate market all but dried up. Even then, Dwayne had managed to maintain a positive outlook.

"You're scaring me."

Dwayne took a breath and squeezed his eyes shut. When he opened them again, he looked directly at Jeremy. "It's your sister."

Jeremy's stomach immediately twisted. Blood rushed from his extremities and he was glad he was sitting, because of the very few times his dad had been upset, there had been one in particular that he remembered clearly. It was when Charlotte, his older sister, had appendicitis and had to have emergency surgery when she was sixteen. That very same look had been on his face then.

"Is she sick? Why wouldn't she tell me?" Charlotte was his senior by two years, but despite the fact that Jeremy was the younger brother, they'd always been close. At least until she'd moved to the East Coast to be with her boyfriend who she'd met online about six months earlier. After she moved, the calls became less and less frequent, and they'd moved most of their communication to text messaging. And lately, even those had stopped.

"What's going on, Dad?"

"That's just it." His dad shook his head. "I'm not sure."

It took a moment for Jeremy to process what he'd said. Or more specifically, what he'd *not* said. "Wait. What? If you don't know what's wrong, then why do you look so upset?" He shook his head and rolled it back, cracking his neck before focusing on his father again. "You need to tell me what the hell is actually going on, Dad. Because I've never seen you look so worked up. Especially if you're *not sure* what's going on."

The older man nodded and cleared his throat. "You know how your mother and I went to visit for Christmas this year?"

"Of course. You said you had a nice time." His parents had decided to go visit Charlotte for Christmas and properly meet her boyfriend Billy while they were there. Jeremy hadn't really asked for a lot of details about the trip because he'd been preoccupied with his own personal life, but what little they had said was positive enough.

"We did." He stopped himself and shook his head. "No. We didn't. When we told you that, it was a lie."

That didn't make any sense and Jeremy said as much. "Why would you lie about your visit?"

"Because we couldn't really make sense of what was happening there and I didn't want to say anything until I knew something for sure. But it just felt *off.* Billy felt off. Their relationship, and…Char didn't seem like herself. She was trying really hard for us to like him and for everything to go perfectly."

That was finally something that made sense. He could absolutely imagine his sister working overtime for their parents to like the man who'd convinced her to quit her job in the city as an interior designer for a busy home builder, and lured her to the other side of the country to work in a coffee shop. Jeremy always thought this Billy must be pretty damn special if Char was willing to give up her career right as it was taking off. But then again, people did all kinds of things for love. Thoughts of Bella popped into his head and he knew in a flash that he would do all kinds of things for her.

But he needed to focus on the situation at hand. "I get that," he said to his dad. "But it was her first Christmas that she hosted in her new home. I'm sure it was stressful for her because she wanted to make it all perfect, right?" Jeremy chuckled. "That doesn't sound odd at all."

"It was, Jeremy." The seriousness in his father's voice cut his laughter off. "Something wasn't right. I couldn't put my finger on it while we were there, and I didn't want to say anything to your mother. I didn't want to worry her, but she noticed it, too. The way Charlotte always kind of looked over her shoulder whenever she was talking to us, as if she didn't know if he was listening. And we were never alone with her. Ever. If we were going to go to the store, he came. If Char and her mom wanted to go for a walk, he'd insist on going, too. It was strange. I just felt like he wasn't quite right."

"But Billy seems like a nice guy." It felt like a stupid thing to say considering Jeremy had never actually met the man. But they'd talked on video calls once or twice when Charlotte had first moved, and Jeremy hadn't noticed anything strange. But now that he thought about it, those calls were a long time ago. Right after Char had moved. They hadn't had a video chat in a long time.

"She doesn't look like herself either," his father continued. "She's lost weight. Her eyes are…" Dwayne couldn't finish the sentence. "We're worried about her."

"What kind of worried?" Jeremy hated asking, afraid of the answer. "Do you think that she's—"

"Trapped." Dwayne pressed his lips together and nodded. "She won't talk to me, Jer. But we don't think she's safe. I need your help."

Bella loaded the last of the boxes they'd filled in the back of her car and slammed the trunk. They'd made a decent amount of progress going through Papa's things. And much to her surprise, he'd been far more agreeable than she'd expected when it came to paring down his belongings.

"They're just things, Bella. The memories are in here." He'd thumped his chest. "You don't need to hold on to a bunch of junk to remember the good times."

His cut-and-dried attitude about it all had taken her off guard, and in a strange twist of events, she'd found herself getting defensive of her grandfather's knickknacks. When he wasn't looking, she pulled a few things out of his donation pile to keep for herself. The crystal candy dish that had always been full of spearmints when she was little was absolutely not going to a thrift shop.

She didn't bother going back into the house to say good-bye before driving her carload. There was no point. Papa had already gone next door to Lydia's. Bella shook her head as she looked in the direction of the neighbor's house. She'd guessed immediately when she'd arrived before Christmas that the older lady was sweet on her grandfather, but for whatever reason, her grandfather had refused to see it.

Seemed as if that situation had changed dramatically. She couldn't help but smile. After all, love happened at any age. She just hoped Papa's new relationship wouldn't interfere with his move to the retirement community they'd finally agreed upon. It had taken way too long to convince her grandfather that he shouldn't live on his own anymore and that just because he moved to a community didn't mean he'd be losing his independence.

But it would mean that he wouldn't accidentally start fires in his kitchen anymore.

Bella chuckled as she got behind the wheel of her car. After all, it was *her*, not her grandfather, who'd started the last fire in his kitchen right before Christmas. Not that it had been entirely her fault. She'd been distracted trying to do too many things at once, and she'd completely forgotten to take the card-board off the frozen lasagna before popping it into the oven.

That situation had turned out pretty good, too. After all, Jeremy had been the firefighter to respond to that call. And if she hadn't started that particular oven fire, who knows whether they would have reconnected again after so many years.

"Everything happens for a reason." She spoke aloud in her tiny car as she backed out of the snowy drive and onto the icy street. She still wasn't totally used to driving on the roads with mounds of snow taller than she was piled up on either side. Glacier Falls was only a few hours out of the city, but being deep in the mountains the way it was, the small town received a lot more snow than Bella was used to. *A lot.*

Jeremy insisted she would get used to driving on snow and ice, and that pretty soon it would be second nature and she wouldn't even think about it. Bella wanted to believe him, but every time she got behind the wheel of her car, she still gripped the steering wheel so tightly she was sure her knuckles were completely white underneath her wooly mittens.

What she hadn't told Jeremy yet was that she wasn't likely to get much practice driving in the winter road conditions over the next few months. Not after the news her agent, Lewis Robson, had called her with late the night before. She'd gotten the movie. *The* movie. The one that she was told would be a massive blockbuster hit. Bella still hadn't fully let herself process the news that she was about to play Zoe, a struggling singer down on her luck who gets discovered and becomes a global sensation almost overnight. The movie was titled *Bomb-shell* and it would involve her not only acting as the protagonist, but also recording almost every song on the soundtrack.

Stephanie had pushed hard for Bella to try out for the role, particularly because she was also starring in the film. She was to play the co-starring role of Veronica—the troubled, drug-addicted star who Bella's character would be displacing from her throne as the world's biggest star. *Bombshell* was set to be gritty but flashy. Emotional, yet uplifting. And the music...Bella didn't even pretend that she wasn't wildly impressed with the lyrics. She was itching to record them and put her voice to the words that would come alive.

The entire project was going to be incredible. Completely life changing. And she'd landed it.

And that equal parts excited her *and* scared the hell out of her.

Bella owed Stephanie Starz more than she could ever repay for the introduction to her agent. Within days of reaching out to him, Lewis had lined up the meetings and auditions that had all led to that moment. Bella had never even considered acting, let alone in giant blockbuster hits.

Everything had happened so fast, more than once Bella found herself getting completely overwhelmed with it all. Thankfully, Stephanie had been more than a good contact to have. She'd been an amazing friend. After New Year's, when Bella went to the city to start taking meetings, Stephanie had been there as well and she'd all but held her hand through it all.

As if just thinking about her new friend had summoned her, Bella's phone chimed with an incoming text message. She glanced down at the phone as she pulled up in front of the thrift shop. With her car safely parked, Bella picked up the phone and read the message.

I decided to come back early, too. Girls night tonight to celebrate? Or are you busy with your sexy firefighter?

Bella laughed and typed her response.

· · ·

I've already been busy. She added the winky emoji and sent it before adding, *Girl's night sounds great. Send me details.*

With Jeremy working, she wouldn't be able to see him again until morning. She might as well go out and have a little fun. Besides, maybe a night of catching up with the ladies of Glacier Falls would be exactly what she needed to take her mind off the news Lewis had given her. It would give her a chance to process it all. She could use as many distractions as possible, especially if they included a night of normalcy. Something that Steph assured her was about to become further and farther between.

The idea made her entire body tingle in excitement and nerves.

Don't mention the movie though, okay?

What? Really?

Steph had been a superstar for so long, Bella was sure she'd forgotten what it was like to be new and unsure.

It would be best if Bella could put it completely out of her mind. At least for one night. Besides, she hadn't even had a chance to tell Jeremy yet. She was going to tell him earlier, but then they'd gotten distracted, *again.* And that seemed far more important than telling him that she wouldn't be spending very much time with him in the foreseeable future.

The idea made her stomach sink. *How would he take the news?*

He'd be happy for her and her success, right?

Of course he would be. Bella was almost certain of it.

Almost.

There was a distinct difference between being happy for someone in theory and really understanding what that meant in reality. And that's what Bella was worried about: the reality of it all. And what it would mean to their brand-new relationship.

Chapter Three

IT HADN'T EVEN BEEN a full year since Stephanie had discovered Glacier Falls and the family she unknowingly had there, but already every time she returned, it felt like coming home. So much had happened since the first time she'd set foot in town, she didn't even feel like the same person.

Probably because she wasn't.

The Stephanie Starz who'd shown up at Ever After Ranch, the gorgeous—and increasingly sought-after—wedding venue run by the Turner twins, Hope and Faith, had been a girl with her priorities in a twist. To say the least. She'd been looking for the perfect place to marry her then-fiancé, Dax Combs, when what she should have been worried about was finding the perfect fiancé. Hers, as it turned out, was far from it.

But it wasn't a total waste of time. Calling off her wedding had opened up space for her sister Faith and her now-husband, Logan, to finally admit their true feelings for each other, get out of their own way and get married themselves. The surprising detail that Hope and Faith were actually Stephanie's half-sisters just made everything so much sweeter. Everything happened for a reason; Stephanie firmly believed that. If it hadn't been for her ill-fated engagement, she never would have come to town, never would have met her half-sisters, and never would have met an entire community that helped her to fill the empty space she'd carried around for most of her life.

She hadn't been entirely truthful with Bella a moment ago when she told her she'd just decided to come home from the city early. Truthfully, she'd always planned to come back a few days early, if everything went according to the plan she'd been working on.

And it had.

Stephanie sat in her SUV, looking out over Lynx Creek, the old fishing village she'd put an offer on right before Christmas. She'd announced it to her friends on Christmas Eve, but it had taken weeks to actually close on the sale.

But now it had. The sale was official, and the little cluster of run-down log cabins and lodges tucked into the trees just on the edge of town was all hers. She wasn't sure whether she should laugh or cry. Or both. Definitely both.

Renovating the buildings and refreshing the property to the point where it could be useable for...what? She still wasn't totally sure. It was a huge project to take on at this point in her life. Or, really, at any point in her life. But when she'd just signed on to co-star in a major production...what had she been thinking?

Stephanie dropped her head and squeezed her eyes shut.

Had she made a mistake?

The buildings were all run-down. Some were falling apart completely. Almost all of them needed new roofs and decks. Never mind the interiors. There was one cabin that was passable but that's only because up until recently it had been inhabited. Still. What *had* she been thinking?

Slowly, she lifted her head and opened her eyes. She kept her breathing slow and regulated as she took in the view outside her windshield. From where she sat, she could only see the main lodge, old cook house, and two of the six sleeping cabins scattered through the tall pine forest. All of which had a thick layer of snow covering them. They looked like frosting-covered gingerbread houses. In fact, the snow helped to make the old camp look far less run-down than it actually was.

A smile crept across her face, and the familiar excitement Stephanie had felt when she'd first set eyes on the property returned with a vengeance.

It was going to be perfect.

And that's why she'd bought it. There was so much potential in the property. All it needed was a little love. A little bit of hard work, time, and care would turn it around. It was going to be amazing.

Unable to contain herself to her vehicle any longer, Stephanie grabbed her mittens, pulled her knit cap down over her full head of red locks, and stepped out of her SUV. Into a snowbank. She laughed at herself as she sank up to her knees in snow.

"Probably should have brought snowshoes." She pulled one leg out and took the biggest step forward she could muster—which wasn't very far given her short legs—and sunk back into the snow.

But a little snow wasn't going to deter her. Not now that the property was officially hers.

It took her far too long to pack down a path to the main lodge building, but once she was in the cover of the trees, there was less excessively deep snow, just the occasional big drift she could skirt around.

Stephanie stamped her feet on the wood deck and immediately regretted it as one of her booted feet broke through a rotten board. "Oh!" Carefully, she pulled her boot out and stepped tentatively over the hole she'd created. "I'll put that on the list."

She chuckled out loud because her list was getting longer

by the second. And not for the first time she considered the sanity in her decision in renovating the existing buildings. It would probably be easier just to bulldoze the entire property and start over.

"But where is the adventure in that?" she said to herself.

Carefully this time, Stephanie walked around the building until she got to the front door, which, to her surprise, still stood fairly solidly in place. She put the old key into the lock and turned, jiggling it just a little before trying the handle. The door moved a little, but the wood had swelled, making it hard to open. She dropped her shoulder and braced herself before pushing hard against the door until it finally moved inward, creaking open.

Stephanie was prepared to find evidence of vandalism or squatters inside. Or more likely, teenagers who'd used the place to party during the summer. It seemed like something she might have done and no doubt some of her new friends would have been just those types of teens when they were younger.

To her shock, there was no evidence of any break-in or vandalism inside. In fact, the lodge building looked as it probably did on the day that the previous owners had locked up and walked away almost fifteen years ago.

There'd been a caretaker on the property up until the winter before, but from what Steph understood, he didn't really have a lot of actual caretaking duties. The previous owner felt a sense of duty to the old man and let him stay on long after her husband died unexpectedly and she'd shuttered the fishing business. Perhaps his presence had served as enough of a deterrent to any potential squatters or partiers?

Either way, it was an added benefit that she didn't have to deal with that on top of what looked like everything else.

The fishing camp was on the other side of Glacier Falls, so one had to drive all the way through town to access it, which meant it wouldn't get a lot of traffic passing by. It was just far enough out to be private and tranquil, but not so far out of town that she'd feel isolated or lonely.

Assuming she made her home there.

It wasn't something she'd thought too much about before. She'd been so preoccupied in what she'd turn the property into that she hadn't considered actually living there when she was in town. She had a home in Los Angeles that, up until recently, she'd spent most of her time in. But more and more, the big city, with the fancy parties and demanding social commitments that came with it, lost its appeal. Being in the mountains had given her a sense of peace that even her hometown, a tiny place of less than five thousand people that her adoptive parents still lived in, couldn't provide.

She walked back outside the lodge to look at the frozen river that in only a few months would thaw and once more spring to life. She could imagine herself sitting in a porch swing, or oversized rocker, in the evenings, listening to the water rush over the rocks. She'd be able to watch deer and maybe even moose right from the very spot in which she stood.

It would be magical.

And just like that, Stephanie couldn't imagine herself living anywhere else.

By the time Stephanie made her way back through town and to the Knot, the local pub and main gathering place for locals, it was already past seven. The place was busier than Stephanie expected it to be for a Thursday night at the beginning of February. Then again, having never spent a winter in Glacier Falls, she really had no idea what to expect. From what she understood from Katie Banks, one of her new friends who'd just opened an adventure shop where she rented out equipment and provided lessons and guided tours, the winter season was starting to become busier than ever as city people discovered the mountains were full of fun activities in all seasons. And her shop, the Hub, was the perfect business to capitalize on that increased traffic and help newbies like Stephanie get outside and try all kinds of new things.

This past summer, she'd tried mountain biking and of course hiking on some of the local trails, but there was still so many things she wanted to check out. And apparently she was going to need to invest in a pair of snowshoes if she planned to go out to her property much more. And she did.

Stephanie crossed the busy room, smiling and waving at a few people she recognized as she made her way to the table in the back, where some of the ladies had already arrived.

Everyone in the room would no doubt recognize her. After all, she was literally one of the biggest stars in Hollywood. At any given time, her face was plastered on at least a dozen different tabloids or magazines. Or more likely, both. Never mind the internet gossip sites that seemed to pop up almost daily with new, interesting, and completely made-up stories about her life. One of her favorite parts about Glacier Falls was that even if she was recognized, almost no one in town would make a big deal about it.

Sure, she might get a handful of people asking for autographs or photos—neither of which she minded. But it was a much more laid-back atmosphere than almost everywhere else in the world she'd been. There was no paparazzi, or big crowds screaming at her, or any of that other stuff that made her want to wear a disguise and hide. In Glacier Falls, she actually just got to be herself.

"Stephanie!"

Faith greeted her with a wave from their usual table in the corner of the busy room. When she got close enough, her sister —something she was still getting used to saying—jumped up and pulled her into a hug. "It's so good to see you. I'm so glad you came back early. Hope is making me crazy. I could use a little backup."

Stephanie laughed and took a seat next to her sister. Hope, Faith's identical twin, was *very* pregnant and on bed rest, a detail that was starting to drive everyone crazy. The sisters ran the busy Ever After wedding event venue, and Steph knew that it was making Hope batty that she couldn't be on her feet, overseeing things for the business she'd started from nothing and had only relinquished to her sister to run. She also knew the situation was making Faith even crazier. "She can't be that bad."

Faith lifted her eyebrows and tilted her head, making Steph laugh harder.

"Okay, okay. She *is* that bad," Steph conceded. "But that's only because she cares so much."

Faith lifted her drink and took a sip. "All I'm saying is that I can't wait for my little niece or nephew to show up because that will give her something else to focus on besides what Logan and I are doing. She wasn't even supposed to be here, for goodness' sake. She didn't seem to care so much when she was traveling all over the world." Faith shook her head again. "I love her, but oh, man…she definitely needs something to keep her busy and out of my hair." She put her glass down and clapped her hands together, refocusing on Steph. "Enough of my bitching. Tell me about you. What's the deal with the movie? Did you take the role? Did Bella get the part?"

Crap. She'd forgotten she'd told her sister about *Bombshell*. And more specifically, that Bella was up for the same movie. Normally, Steph would be more than happy to discuss the details of the film and the shooting schedule and anything else her sister wanted to know. But for whatever reason, Bella had asked her not to mention it.

"About that," she started. "I told Bella I wouldn't mention the movie or—"

"What movie?" Sarah Morris and her sister-in-law, Nicole, appeared.

Double crap.

"Steph was just telling me about this amazing new movie, *Bombshell*, she's going to be involved in." Faith looked at Steph and clarified, "You *are* going to be involved, right? I mean, you took the role…" Steph nodded slowly and Faith turned back to the other women. "And Bella was auditioning for the lead role in the same film. Pretty cool, right? To think that—"

"I just don't think we should talk about it tonight." Steph tried to keep her voice casual. "I mean, it's not that exciting or—"

"Not exciting?" Sarah all but fell into the chair next to her. "Are you kidding, Steph?" She shook her head with a chuckle. "You do know that I have a six-year-old, right? Between work and playdate dramas, I could use something *actually* exciting in my life. Even if it means just living vicariously through you. And come on, Steph. You really are the most exciting person I know." Sarah waved a hand around the table. "No offense to the rest of you."

"No offense taken here." Nicole shrugged. "Besides Amy telling me some gossip from the restaurant when she gets home, my life is bor-ing."

"Honestly." Steph shook her head. "I really don't think I should say anything." Movement by the door caught her eye, and she looked up to see Bella walk into the bar. "I'm sure you all understand that it's not really my news to talk about—"

"News?" Sarah jumped on her word choice. "You mean there's actually news about *Bombshell*?"

"Steph's in it for sure," Faith jumped in. "So that's news. I don't know about Bella, but—"

"Bella what?" The topic of the conversation herself appeared at the table and shrugged her coat off. "What about me?"

Steph watched Bella look around the table. Her eyes landed on her in question, but it was Nicole who said, "We were just wondering about this new movie and—"

"You told them I got the part?"

"No! I didn't—"

"You got it?"

"No way!"

"Oh my God!"

Everyone spoke at once and jumped up from their seats to pull Bella into hugs. There was so much cheering and excitement that it took a moment for Steph to see clearly through the group to her friend. Bella looked shell-shocked by the unexpected attention, certainly. But she also looked happy. Happy and excited and more than anything, that made Steph happy.

It was a big deal to get your first movie role. Let alone your first role in a major blockbuster production. She *should* be ecstatic.

As soon as the women settled down, took their seats, and ordered a round of drinks to celebrate, Steph caught Bella's eye. "I didn't say anything."

Bella shrugged. "It's okay. It's not going to be a secret for too much longer. It's just…" She lifted her shoulders in a shrug. "I didn't have a chance to tell Jeremy yet."

"Jer doesn't know?"

Bella looked at Faith, who'd asked the question. She confirmed that no, she hadn't had a chance to tell him yet.

"I get it now," Faith said apologetically. "I'm sorry I pushed. I can be like that sometimes. A little too pushy for my own good."

Steph tried not to laugh when Sarah agreed with an emphatic nod.

Faith ignored her and kept talking. "Okay, we won't say anything. Right, girls?" She waited until Nicole and Sarah both nodded in agreement. "You need to be the one to tell him. It's pretty major news and it's your news to tell."

"That's right," Sarah agreed. "Your secret is safe with us."

Bella looked noticeably relieved and thanked them all as a round of drinks showed up. Steph led them in a toast, and they drank to Bella's success.

When the toast was over, Faith put her drink down on the table in front of her and very seriously steepled her fingers together as she looked at Bella. "Now, I think everyone is waiting for some details about a certain sexy firefighter, Bella. What exactly is going on between the two of you?"

"Yes," Sarah joined in. "We want *all* the details."

She wiggled her eyebrows as Bella groaned and the group dissolved into giggles.

Chapter Four

IF THERE WAS something better than a fresh out of the oven cinnamon bun from Sweetie Pies, Bella didn't know what it was. She closed her eyes as she bit into the flaky pastry and let the burst of cinnamon and sugar fill her mouth. It may not be the healthiest choice for breakfast, but it was certainly the most delicious and she planned to enjoy every single moment of her treat.

Particularly because now that she was supposed to be playing the part of a sex symbol in *Bombshell*, she would definitely not be able to eat like this for a while. Steph had filled Bella in on all the restricted diets her nutritionists and trainers put her on for various roles over the years. The one thing they all had in common was that they absolutely did not include freshly baked cinnamon buns.

"Mmmm." Bella took another bite and took her time savoring it.

"Wow. I wish I could make you that happy."

Bella's eyes flew open at the sound of Jeremy's voice. She let out a little squeal of happiness and, cinnamon bun forgotten, she jumped up and threw herself in his arms. She pressed a kiss to his lips. "You make me even happier than a pastry ever could. Although...this one comes pretty close."

"Yum." He touched a finger to his mouth. "Your kisses are always pretty sweet, but that was next level."

Bella swatted him playfully and sat again, pulling her plate closer. "I would share, but..."

"It's a Sweetie Pies cinnamon bun." His face shifted into a mask of seriousness. "And everyone knows, you don't share a Sweetie Pies cinnamon bun." He cracked into a smile. "Give me a second, I'll be right back. Do you want anything?"

She shook her head and watched as Jeremy went to the counter to order his breakfast.

It never failed to impress Bella the way that everyone in town knew him and genuinely liked him. Everywhere they went, people called out to Jeremy and greeted him with hugs and friendly slaps on the back. It filled Bella with pride to see the way Jeremy was respected and loved as a son of Glacier Falls.

She watched now as he chatted with the woman behind the counter. She was still pretty new to town, so Bella was still meeting people and trying to learn names and keep people straight. She couldn't remember what the woman's name was, but like almost everyone else, she obviously knew Jeremy. And liked him. That much was clear by the way she tilted her head and giggled at whatever it was he was saying to her. Even from where she sat, Bella could see that the other woman was batting her eyelashes at him and sending out all kinds of *I'm available* vibes.

But he wasn't available.

He was hers. It was something she was still getting used to, but she liked it. It felt right.

Even with her history of a past boyfriend cheating on her with pretty much every woman he saw, Bella never had been the jealous type, which was going to work out well considering they were about to be spending a lot of time apart.

The smile on her face dimmed.

She'd had a good time with the ladies the night before, and Steph was right—they *did* need to celebrate. But she couldn't help feeling guilty that she hadn't told Jeremy yet. She'd managed to put it out of her mind, but now watching him and the lady behind the counter flirting so shamelessly with him, she couldn't help but get a little bit worried with how he'd react.

She was still watching when the woman behind the counter winked at him as she handed him his order. Bella shook her head with a little internal laugh because he was completely oblivious to her attentions. She focused on her cinnamon bun again. She wasn't worried about Jeremy being interested in anyone else. The connection between the two of them was special.

When they were together, it was magic.

Just thinking about being alone with Jeremy send thrills through her body and completely distracted her from any worry she held. The feeling with him was unlike any she had ever had. And it didn't take an expert in love and relationships to know that that was special.

Just like the cinnamon bun in front of her.

The comparison made her giggle.

And she was still giggling when Jeremy returned to the table with a pastry of his own and a coffee in his hand.

"What's got you laughing? It's not me, is it?"

She couldn't help it; as soon as she looked up into his eyes, Bella burst into a fit of giggles again. "No." She tried to look as serious as possible as she shook her head. "Of course not."

Jeremy gave her an unbelieving look.

"Well," Bella continued. "Okay. Maybe a little." She pulled

a piece of her breakfast off and held it up. "I was just thinking that you were a lot like this cinnamon bun."

He chuckled but took the bait as he tore a piece of his own bun off and put it in his mouth. "Oh yeah? And how is that?"

Bella tilted her head and examined the sugary pastry. "Well," she began. "You're both pretty sweet." She paused and moved her head to the other shoulder. "And of course, you are both quite delicious." She worked hard not to laugh. "But most importantly, you're a *very* special treat that I look forward to when I come to town." She popped the piece in her mouth and closed her eyes as she enjoyed it thoroughly.

Bella knew when she opened her eyes Jeremy would be watching her, and she wasn't disappointed. He looked at her with an intensity that sent a whole new type of thrill through her body.

"Well, I'll tell you what...I know I certainly could get used to this type of sweetness every day."

Her laughter died, and a flash of worry shot through her at his choice of words.

Every day?

Surely Jeremy must know that they couldn't have an everyday relationship.

Not now. Not with her career just taking off. There were so many factors to consider. So many things that were about to happen.

Which meant she'd be in the city, working, and Jeremy would be...here.

Unless he went with her.

No. Bella chastised herself for entertaining the thought, even for a second.

It was way too soon. Ridiculously soon to be thinking that way. Jeremy wasn't going to travel with her while she was working. That didn't make any sense. Especially because they hadn't even declared themselves a formal couple. Hell, she didn't even use the word boyfriend yet. She couldn't expect him to uproot his entire life to follow her around. That was beyond selfish. She'd never ask it of him.

Bella swallowed hard. She was overthinking things, and she needed to stop it before her train of thoughts got away from her completely.

"Whoa." Jeremy had put his breakfast down and watched her intently. "What is going on in that head of yours? Did I say something wrong?"

Her brain spun and Bella forced herself to focus. She smiled sweetly. "You wouldn't want too much of a good thing, though, would you?"

It was ridiculous to even let herself think about this at all.

She needed to take things slow. She needed to focus on her career, and enjoy whatever it was that was happening between her and Jeremy. And she would not overthink it.

Jeremy was the best man she'd met in a very long time—maybe ever—and she was determined not to screw it up by overthinking it or moving too quickly. No. She'd take things slowly this time and do it right. She was determined.

He opened his mouth to answer, but Bella beat him to it before he could say what she knew he would. "I got the part."

"What?" He sat back in shock and she watched his reaction closely.

She hoped and prayed he was happy for her. Excited for what it meant for her. For her career. Bella watched for a flicker of disappointment in his eyes, or anything that would tell her that he wasn't just as excited as she was.

There was nothing but happiness there.

It obviously took him a moment to process what she'd said, and when it registered, Jeremy's mouth fell open. He reached across the table, almost knocking their coffees over, and took her hand. "You got the part?"

She nodded.

"*The* part?"

She nodded again.

"The part that...*Bombshell?*"

She nodded a third time. This time, tears came to her eyes and she blinked hard to keep them at bay.

"I did." Her voice was soft, barely audible. But Jeremy heard it.

"Holy shit, Bella!" Jeremy squeezed her hands and then he was up and out of his chair. He pulled her into a hug, lifting her off the ground as he spun her around in the small coffee shop. "This is amazing. Congratulations, babe!"

When he set her down again, he spent a second apologizing to the people he'd almost hit when he'd spun her, but then proudly announced to the room, "She got the part! My girlfriend, Bella Burton, is going to be *the* Bombshell."

Girlfriend. The word sounded good and only made his proclamation all the sweeter. She let herself bask in the glow of his attention and for the first time allowed herself to be happy about everything that was happening. *Really* happy.

Everything was going to be okay.

No.

It was going to be better than okay. Because she had the best boyfriend in the whole world *and* all her career dreams were about to come true. Nothing could be better.

———

Despite his lack of sleep the night before, it had been a great day. Jeremy was used to not getting a full night's sleep, and he would normally spend much of the next day in bed, recharging and resting. But spending his day with Bella was an even better way to rejuvenate. He felt as if he'd never have to sleep again if it meant spending more time with her.

He was completely lovestruck, and he loved every single minute of it.

After her announcement, Jeremy would have happily taken Bella straight home and directly into his bed to celebrate in their own, very special way. But he managed to muster enough self-control to wait and give her a special day to mark the occasion. After all, it wasn't every day that your girlfriend—a label he was more than happy to finally start using—landed a starring role in a major film production.

After the bakery, they'd walked down the street to the Hub, where Katie had set them up with some fat tired bikes, perfect for riding the trails around town in the snow. Glacier Falls had an extensive trail system right in town that went down along the river and the waterfalls, which were mostly frozen this time of year. The water still flowed under the ice, and it was pretty awesome to hear the power of the water moving even if you couldn't see it.

Katie had just brought in the fat tire bikes, and Jeremy hadn't had a chance to try them yet. Mostly because they were almost always rented out. The activity had become super popular, and Jeremy had to call in a favor from his old friend to reserve the bikes especially for them. It was a favor that only a few months ago Katie never would have agreed to. Sure, they were old friends, but they also used to be a bit of an item—if you could call it that—and when Katie had up and married her best friend Damon Banks in what turned out to originally be a fake wedding, to say that Jeremy had been caught off guard would have been an understatement.

No one had been more surprised than he was to find out about the wedding, let alone the fact that it turned out Katie and Damon had always had feelings for each other. Jeremy, of course, hadn't been thrilled about feeling like a fool, and he may have punched out Damon, who was also an old friend. But that was all before he'd really understood that the feelings the two of them had for each other were real. And unlike anything Jeremy and Katie had ever had for each other. Far from it.

It wasn't really until he'd reconnected with Bella that Jeremy fully understood how different it was to be completely and totally in love with someone.

At any rate, Katie and Jeremy had made peace and finally, they were all back to normal and able to once again be friends. And, as luck would have it, it paid to have a friend who would reserve the hottest equipment in town for him.

Katie set them up with the bikes, promising them it was "just like riding a bike" and it was. Only better. Because these bikes and their oversized tires had extra grip and made it easy and fun to ride on the snow and ice.

He'd been pleased and impressed that Bella had been just as keen to give the bikes a try.

Thankfully, the cold snap of a week ago was gone, and for February, it wasn't too cold. They were bundled up appropriately in layers they had to take off as they got their heart rates up, pushing each other to go faster and farther, laughing the entire time. The fresh air and exercise had done Jeremy good, too. It didn't take long before his mind felt clearer; he was wide awake and not only could he completely enjoy himself with Bella, but he could also sort out a few thoughts about his sister.

The night before, after his dad unloaded his concerns and fears about Charlotte on to him, any chance Jeremy had of getting a bit of sleep between emergency calls was all but lost. He'd tossed and turned for hours, trying to figure out what was going on with his big sister and why she wouldn't say anything to him. They were close.

Charlotte was a strong woman. It just didn't make sense. There was no way his big sister would ever allow herself to be in an abusive relationship of any kind.

It didn't make any sense.

His mom and dad had to have it wrong.

By the time he'd finally given up on trying to get any rest and pulled himself out of the bunk he used to crash in at the station, it was too late to call Charlotte, especially with the time change on the East Coast. Instead, he sent a text that she would get first thing in the morning.

Sis. What's up? Everything good out there with you?

He sent the message and clicked off his phone, not expecting a reply until morning. The simple act of reaching out and sending the text had given him some peace. Besides, Charlotte was fine. He knew it.

Sometimes he thought maybe his mom and dad were just looking for something to worry about. Maybe they needed a new hobby now that they were retired. It was entirely likely that they just had too much time on their hands.

In the morning before meeting up with Bella, he checked his phone and there was no new message from his sister. But there was a notification that Charlotte had seen the message. She was probably just busy. He wouldn't worry about it. Not yet.

And he hadn't. At least not for a few hours while he was riding bikes around town with Bella. She'd turned out to be the perfect distraction.

He couldn't remember the last time he'd had so much fun.

Except he could. Anytime he'd spent with her had been fun. When they'd gone together to get a Christmas tree for her to share with her grandfather, and then when they'd visited Ever After Ranch and the Christmas festivities they'd had, including the sleigh ride. That had also been an amazing day.

Pretty much all of his days with Bella were fantastic. And

there was no way Jeremy could ever see that changing. Except, now that she'd be busy working, those fantastic times might get a little further apart.

For a bit.

Not forever, he told himself.

He hadn't been surprised when Bella told him the news. He'd known she was going to get the part. Well, maybe not that specific part. But Jeremy had known something would come up. A record deal, a movie part—something. Bella was way too talented for it to *not* happen. And he *had* been genuinely thrilled for her. Of course he was; her dreams were coming true. What kind of asshole would he be if he wasn't excited for her?

A selfish asshole who wanted to keep her close.

A sliver of doubt tried to work its way into his consciousness and just as quickly, Jeremy forced it away. He couldn't let his thoughts go there. He glanced behind him on the bike to see Bella, her hair streaming out from under her knit cap, a huge smile on her face as she pedaled behind him. She was looking over at the river and didn't notice him watching her.

She looked happier than he'd ever seen her.

And why wouldn't she? It was all coming together for her.

She deserved it all.

Even if it meant that it might be a little bit hard on him. But it wasn't about him. It was all about Bella.

When they'd had enough of riding around town, they ventured a little farther out to the trails in the trees. The snow in the woods was a little deeper, and the trails definitely provided more challenging terrain, but by then they were both up to the challenge. They pushed themselves through the winter wonderland until finally they were exhausted and couldn't take any more.

They dropped their bikes off at the Hub and stopped quickly at the grocery store to grab the makings for a charcuterie board, along with a bottle of wine, before heading back to his small apartment as the sun started to set.

He'd contemplated taking Bella out to Birchwood for a proper celebration, where no doubt owner Brody Morris would make them something amazing and delish for the occasion. But Jeremy was feeling selfish and he wanted a little bit of alone time with her.

Jeremy looked up from the cutting board where he'd been slicing meats and cheeses when Bella walked into the living room.

He put the knife down and let out a low whistle of appreciation.

She'd changed out of her winter gear into some simple black leggings and an oversized sweatshirt that slipped seductively off her shoulder. With her dark hair falling down in soft waves and her cheeks pink from the wind and the sun of the day, Jeremy couldn't remember her ever looking so beautiful.

"You look gorgeous." He walked around the kitchen counter so he could pull her into his arms and kiss her.

Her lips were soft against his, and she melted into his touch, but only for a moment. "Jeremy, you're being ridiculous. I'm wearing leggings, for God's sakes. I hardly look—"

"Like the most beautiful woman I've ever seen." He cut her off with another kiss. This time, he pulled her closer so she couldn't slip away and cupped a hand on her cheek, letting his thumb stroke the soft skin there. "You could be wearing a burlap sack, and I'd still think you were the most gorgeous woman in the world. In fact, it doesn't matter what you're wearing at all." He wiggled his eyebrows playfully. "Oh, I like the idea of you wearing nothing at all."

Bella smacked his arm playfully and pushed out of his embrace. "Down, boy." She reached for the glass of wine he'd poured her and lifted it in a toast. "There'll be time for that later."

Jeremy's groin tightened in anticipation of exactly what would be happening later.

Bella made him feel things he had never felt before. Not with anyone. The feeling still caught him off guard sometimes. He'd never even known it was possible to feel so drawn to another human being before. It would have been a little unsettling if it didn't feel so amazing.

He lifted his own wineglass and clinked it to hers. "To you and to *Bombshell*," he started. "I am so proud of you, and I know you're going to be absolutely amazing." Bella smiled softly and moved to lift her glass, but he wasn't done. "And to us," he added. "And being together again. Which is my very favorite thing." He smiled, although he couldn't help but notice that her smile faded a little.

Did he say something wrong?

Before he could ask her about it, the smile was back on her face. She clinked glasses with him. "To us." And they drank.

"So," Jeremy moved back into the kitchen to finish preparing the charcuterie board, "are you going to tell me all the details about the movie? It's so crazy. I expected you to get a record deal, sure. But a movie?"

"I know, right?" She moved to the couch and watched him while he finished the preparations of their snack. "I didn't really expect it either. But when Lewis told me about the movie, and the chance to perform the soundtrack, too…it was too good." Her face took on a flurry of excitement. "And, Jer, wait until you see the script. It's so good. I mean, the fact that they'd consider a total unknown to play this role…" She exhaled a deep breath and shook her head in wonder. "It's all so overwhelming."

He arranged some crackers next to the meats and cheeses, opened a jar of hot pepper jelly he'd picked up at a specialty store, and took the tray over to the couch where Bella was reclining.

"You're going to be great, babe." Jeremy selected a piece of brie and paired it with a slice of hot Genoa. He put it on a cracker and held it out to her. "I know it's a lot, but you were born to be a star." She nodded, and he popped the cracker into her open, waiting mouth before she could answer.

She made a small moan of approval as she ate her snack. "I hope you're right," she said when she was done eating. "And thank you for being so supportive, Jeremy. It feels pretty good to have my *boyfriend*…" She looked at him from the corner of her eye as she tried out the word for the first time.

He couldn't help but grin so wide it hurt. The word sounded damn good.

"Be so supportive," she continued. "It really does help to know you've got my back, Jer. Really."

"Oh, Bella. I have your back all day long." He couldn't help it. There was no way he could pass up the opportunity. Jeremy put the cracker he was holding down, and shimmied closer to her on the couch. He lifted himself so he hovered over her. "And I'll have your front and…"

She laughed and pushed him away playfully. "Yeah, yeah. But right now I'm starving."

Jeremy kissed her quickly before moving back to his seat with a small bounce. "Okay, I'll let you eat," he said with a laugh. "But only because I have full intentions to see both your back *and* your front later."

Bella's face pinked, and she looked down into her glass of wine.

He loved the fact that he could make her blush like that. She was usually so composed from years of performing—he liked the fact that he could make her crack. Even just a little.

And it was a small thing, but she was going to have to get used to all types of attention when she was famous. The thought hit him all at once. *Bella was going to be famous.* He was sure of it. There was a reason that Stephanie Starz had hooked her up with her agent. Bella had star power. Everyone could see it. And now that she'd landed this breakout role...her star was definitely going to rise quickly. The thought filled him with pride. And if he was completely honest, it also made him nervous.

What would it mean for them?

"We'll see about that," Bella teased, bringing Jeremy back into the moment. "But let's not talk about the movie anymore." She waved her hand a little, dismissing the topic. "I just want to focus on being here, back in Glacier Falls, with you." She blew him a kiss. "The last few weeks have been so insane, I just want to relax, and enjoy myself."

"And move Roy into his new place?" Jeremy couldn't help but grin. Bella had been working on him for ages and at Christmas, he'd finally agreed to move. Which was great. What was not so great was that Bella had likely underestimated how much work it would be to move the old man out of the home he had lived in for so long.

She groaned and leaned her head back against the couch. "He has so much stuff." She shook her head with a chuckle before making herself another cracker with meat and cheese.

"You know I'll help as much as I can," Jeremy said. "I have a few days off coming up. Just tell me what you need."

While they were talking, he'd once again shifted closer to her on the couch so his hand could rest on her thigh. Now, it was slowly making its way up her leg. He had been patient long enough.

"You know I'll take you up on that offer of help. But," she added, "I heard from my mom too. She's decided to come to town to help as well."

Jeremy's hand paused. He looked at her with a question in his eyes. "Does that mean I get to meet your mother?"

She nodded, a tiny smile on her face.

Meeting the parents was a big step in a relationship. Not that he was in any way nervous about it. In fact, nothing about Bella and their new relationship made him nervous. Nothing.

Everything about her, and them, and what they could be together, excited him.

He took a deep breath, inhaling slowly. As he exhaled, he leaned close to her and pressed a kiss on her neck, just behind her ear.

He moved slowly, leaving a trail of kisses down toward her sweatshirt as his hands worked their way up and under the hem of the oversized fabric. Yes, absolutely everything about Bella excited him.

Chapter Five

ANY AND ALL thoughts about anything except for the way Jeremy's lips on Bella's skin caused her entire body to spark with desire were forgotten as he began to move against her.

Bella dropped her head back against the cushions of the sofa, giving Jeremy better access to her neck. Access he immediately took advantage of.

"Mmm, that feels good." She melted further into the couch.

Their snack board forgotten, Jeremy moved so he straddled over her. "*You* feel good. I seriously cannot get enough of you, Bella."

He dropped his mouth to hers again. This time the kiss was deeper, more urgent.

Her own need flooded through her. She arched her back up to press her breasts into his chest.

"Still too many layers." Jeremy's hands slipped up and under her sweatshirt again. This time, they lifted the fabric up and off her head. He took a sharp gasp of air as her naked breasts were revealed to him.

When she'd changed earlier, she hadn't bothered with a bra, and his reaction was totally worth it.

"You have the most perfect breasts." Jeremy scooped one in each hand and cupped them before lowering his mouth to first one nipple and then the next. He gave them equal attention, sucking and nipping until Bella squirmed beneath him.

"Jeremy." His name was little more than a moan on her lips, but he didn't relent in his attentions.

The heat between her legs grew. She could feel her panties moisten as her legs began to quake. But still, he didn't slow.

"Jeremy." She said his name with more urgency this time, although she couldn't be sure what she was asking from him. Definitely not to stop. But also not to...

Moments before an orgasm crashed through her, he pulled away, leaving her breathless against the cushions. Jeremy sat back with a small, self-satisfied smile on his face. She had never before come from such attentions. But Jeremy...he just had a way about him that fired up every single one of her senses and pushed her into overdrive. The sex with him had been incredible from the very first touch.

It took her a moment to come back to her senses, and recover from the unexpected orgasm. But only a moment. Maybe she was greedy, but she didn't care. She was far from done with him.

Bella took a deep breath, reached out, and tugged at his T-shirt.

"It's like that, is it?"

She licked her bottom lip, taking extra satisfaction in the way Jeremy's pupils dilated at the sight of her. "It is *very* much like that."

Thankfully, he didn't need much encouragement. Jeremy shed himself of his shirt before standing in front of her on the couch. Next, she watched as he unbuckled his jeans and pushed them down to the floor, along with his boxer briefs, leaving him perfectly, gloriously naked in front of her.

"Ummm," she groaned. "That's what I'm talking about." She crooked her finger and beckoned him to her. "Now get back here."

"Oh baby, that's exactly what I plan on doing." But instead of rejoining her on the couch, Jeremy bent and tugged at her leggings.

She wiggled in an effort to help him remove the garment, but they were not coming off easily. The fabric clung to the backs of her thighs, a situation that only seemed to get worse as he struggled with them.

"Did you glue these on? Holy shit." Jeremy laughed and tugged harder, causing Bella to slide further down the couch.

She caught herself before falling off completely but she couldn't stop herself from laughing. "Easy, tiger. Or I'm going to end up on the floor."

He paused his removal of her clothing and narrowed his eyes in desire. "Baby, I'll happily take you on the floor if it means I can finally get you naked."

The flare of need in his eyes sent a shot of desire directly to her core.

The leggings needed to come off. *Now.*

With Bella's help, and a little more pulling, Jeremy managed to finally divest her of the leggings. She'd managed to stay on the couch, but finally, mercifully, she was completely naked and by this time, almost desperate with need. But Jeremy still wasn't moving. Instead, he stood directly in front of her, watching her with that intense gaze of his that just drove her even more crazy and made her want him even more. If it was possible.

"Jeremy." Her voice held a warning tone. A warning for what, she couldn't be sure because she had no idea what she would do if she *didn't* have him. And soon. The only thought swirling through her brain was how badly she needed this man. *Now.*

Still, he didn't move.

"Jeremy?" she said again. She was starting to get concerned. *Why hadn't he moved? Did he not want her? Had he changed his mind?* No. There was no way. She knew exactly what kind of effect she had on the man. Because he had exactly the same one on her. Still, he just stood there, staring at her with an unreadable expression in his eyes. "Jer!"

In a flash, whatever spell was over him broke. He shook his head slightly, snapping out of whatever trance he was in. A sexy grin played on his lips, and finally, mercifully, he stepped toward her. "Sorry, baby. I was just thinking about how lucky I was that I was about to sleep with Hollywood's next biggest star."

She couldn't help it—a full body blush spread over her bare skin. Judging by the flare in his nostrils, Jeremy had noticed it too.

"And now, I'm just enjoying the view."

She shook her head, bit her bottom lip hard and once more crooked her finger to beckon him to her. "Get over here. I'm getting impatient."

Mercifully, he didn't have to be asked again. Jeremy moved swiftly. He grabbed a condom from the pocket of his jeans and in only a few quick moves sheathed himself before he bent down to scoop her up off the couch.

Bella squealed a little at the surprise, but quickly wrapped her legs around him, and hung on tight. "Take me to bed, handsome."

"No time." He bent and kissed her hard before turning around and dropping backward onto the couch with Bella still straddling his lap.

She licked her lips and took her time to let her tongue travel the length on her bottom lip, enjoying the look on Jeremy's face. Need for her blazed in his eyes. It was a giddy power she held over him. A power that was reflected one thousand percent in her own need for him.

Without another word, he lifted her easily by the hips and brought her down slowly so she sheathed his throbbing, hard erection with her warmth. She closed her eyes, let her head drop backward, and groaned as he filled her completely.

Yes. That's exactly where he belonged. Where *she* belonged. With him. Just like this.

"Damn, woman." His voice came out on a breath. "You feel absolutely amazing."

"Mmm." She lifted her head so she could look into his eyes as she started to move.

He groaned and closed his eyes for a moment, a small, satisfied smile working at the edge of his mouth.

As she moved, Bella's climax built quickly. It wasn't going to take much for her to come apart. She increased her pace as the tingling that had begun to build in her core started traveling outward and—

Jeremy's hands clamped down on her hips, stilling her. "I'm going to need a minute."

Bella shook her head. "Oh no, there will be no minute."

"Babe." He pressed his lips together. "I'm sorry, you're just so…I need—"

She bent to his mouth and kissed him deep and hard until his hands left her hips and moved to her back, pulling her closer as she once again resumed the rocking motion that propelled them both quickly into shattering orgasms.

———

Reveling in the aftermath of what had been his most intense climax since…well, the last time he was with Bella, Jeremy pulled her closer against his chest and inhaled the sweetness of her. If Jeremy could have Bella in his arms like this forever, he would die a happy man. There was literally nothing else in his life he needed, as long as he had her this way.

Or any way at all.

It should scare him how quickly he was falling in love with her, but it didn't. It just felt right. Like they could handle anything together.

He nuzzled into the back of her neck and she snuggled in with a groan of satisfaction. He closed his eyes and breathed in the scent of her.

No. He wasn't scared of the way he was feeling. Not even a little bit.

The idea made him smile. Because as crazy as it *should* feel, it didn't.

Bella was his missing piece.

Reluctantly, Jeremy shifted on the couch so he was sitting up and Bella was next to him. He reached down and grabbed the blanket that had slipped to the floor and pulled it up over them.

As if she'd read his mind, Bella sighed as she snuggled into him again. "I could get used to this."

"I absolutely agree. This feels like paradise." It wasn't an exaggeration. Having her bare skin pressed up against his was like the best kind of paradise. His own perfect version. And one he would quite happily stay in as long as he possibly could.

He chuckled under his breath, completely aware that he was over-romanticizing the moment.

"What's so funny?" Bella tipped her head up to look at him.

Jeremy brushed a strand of hair off her forehead and gazed into her eyes. "If I tell you, you'll laugh, too. Only you'll be laughing *at* me."

"Tell me. I won't laugh at you. I promise."

"That is definitely not a promise you're going to be able to keep." Jeremy shook his head. Without a doubt she was going to laugh at him, but he didn't care. Not really. "But I'll tell you anyway."

Bella shifted so she sat up a little bit more, and Jeremy instantly missed the feel of her hot skin on his. He had to resist the urge to pull her back into him.

"Okay, you're going to think I'm ridiculous, but I was just thinking how perfect this all is. You. Me. Here like this. Like it was always meant to be. Like we were always meant to reconnect after all these years and be together. It's like...fate."

To Jeremy's surprise, she didn't laugh at him. In fact, she didn't even smile. Instead, with complete seriousness, she looked at him intently. "And why do you think that was so funny?" There was a question in her eyes. "Because, it seems to me, that that's actually a pretty nice thought."

"You think so, do you?"

"Sure." She nodded. "I love being here with you, too. Why did you think I'd laugh at you?"

"It's hard to explain." He shrugged, no longer quite so self-conscious. "It's just when I'm with you, you make me feel like I've never felt before. Hell, I've always been the tough guy, Bella. The firefighter. The rugged mountain man. But with you...I'm all romantic and poetic or something, and I don't know how to be that guy." He laughed again and waited for her to join in. When she didn't, he asked, "You don't think it's ridiculous?"

Bella shook her head. "I think it's sweet. *Really* sweet." She traced her finger along his arm. "And maybe you don't think you know how to be that guy, but you *are* that guy and I, for one, really like him."

"You do, do you?"

She nodded slowly. "And...I feel the same. This *is* amazing. Being with you always is. Sometimes I wish I could transport

you, so that you're in the city with me all the time or on set…
I'm going to miss you."

Miss you.

She finally laughed, but it was Jeremy's turn to get serious.
The smile fell off his lips as he processed exactly what she'd
just said. She was going to *miss* him?

"Jer?"

He turned away, aware that he needed to say something,
but having no idea at all what it was he could say that could
properly express how he was feeling. Especially because he had
no idea how he *was* feeling.

She was leaving. Right. He knew that logically. Of course he
did. When she told him she'd gotten the role, Jeremy had
known that it meant she had to leave Glacier Falls and go back
to the city, or LA or wherever it was that they shot movies like
that. Of course. But as much as he *knew* it, he hadn't *thought*
about it. And he definitely hadn't thought about what it might
mean to them.

Her hand reached out and touched his shoulder. It was a
tentative touch, as if she were unsure, and he hated that he was
making her feel in any way unsure about him or his feelings for
her. He *hated* it. But despite that, he couldn't bring himself to
say the things she needed to hear. Mostly because he had no
idea what that was.

His mind spun. His heart was in his throat and for a few
minutes, it was hard to breathe.

"Jeremy?" She shook him a little. "You're worrying me."
She gently and firmly turned him so he was looking at her
again. "Say something. Anything."

He knew that right then, whatever it was he said, it could
make or break the moment.

It took a ridiculous amount of effort, but Jeremy dug deep,
took a breath in, and exhaled slowly, with a smile he hoped
reached his eyes. "Sorry," he said slowly. "I'm not trying to

worry you. You just took me off guard is all." He took another breath and on that exhale, shook off the worry that had started to settle over him. "I'm going to miss you, too."

He hoped like hell it was the right thing to say because it was without a doubt the biggest understatement that had ever crossed his lips.

It took a moment, but a sparkle slowly returned to her eyes and a smile to her lips. "You are?"

"You know I am." He took her hand in his and twined his fingers through hers. "I would go with you if I could."

"You should!" She jumped up and flipped her hair over her shoulder. "Come with me. That's a great idea. We could explore LA and the beaches. Maybe we could even go to Disney—"

"Bella." He interrupted her softly. "You know I can't do that, right?"

The light in her eyes dimmed a little.

"My life is in Glacier Falls, Bella. I can't just drop everything and come with you."

She dropped her chin to her chest. "I know."

"Hey." Jeremy reached out, put one finger gently on her chin, and tilted her head up so she looked at him again. "It's okay, Bella. We'll make it work. Besides, absence makes the heart grow fonder, right?"

He didn't believe a word of what he was saying, but maybe if he said it with enough enthusiasm they'd both start to believe.

An unshed tear pooled in the corner of her eye.

"Hey," he said quickly, desperately hoping to keep her from crying. "Do not cry," he commanded. "There is absolutely nothing to cry about. We should be celebrating. *Bombshell* is going to be huge and then you'll be such a big movie star you can be like Steph and make your home right here in Glacier Falls and we can always be together."

Even if he wasn't buying into what he was saying—and he wasn't—Bella seemed to be. And that's all that mattered. He'd sort his own feelings out later.

"Do you believe me?"

She hesitated, but finally nodded. "Okay."

"Okay?" He laughed. "Good." Jeremy leaned forward and pressed a quick kiss to her nose. "Because I'm never wrong."

She smacked him playfully and with the serious moment dissolved, Jeremy let the blanket fall away as he stood and reached for his clothes. He needed a drink.

"Would you like some more wine?" He turned, the glass in his hand already, and saw her nod.

Jeremy handed it to her. The last thing he'd wanted or expected was to have their evening take such a serious turn. He must remember that he needed to go easy. They were still new and their relationship was about to face a major challenge that most didn't have to deal with, especially so early on.

"Do you know what I think?" He worked hard to keep his voice light and fun, exactly the way he wanted the rest of the evening to go. "I think we should toast. To us."

Bella laughed. "You already toasted to us."

"I don't think it can hurt to do it again." He winked. "Besides, we're pretty awesome. And we're going to keep being awesome throughout it all. I'm so excited for you."

She clinked her glass to his. "Thank you for being supportive, Jeremy. I really appreciate it. All of this is so new and exciting, but also really scary and totally overwhelming all at the same time." She took a sip of her wine and held it in her mouth before speaking again. "Thank you."

He paused, his own glass halfway to his lips. "You don't have to thank me, Bella. I couldn't dream of being any other way."

She moved so quickly, he almost spilled his wine all over the couch as she launched into his arms, but he caught her without spilling a drop. Her lips tasted sweet like wine.

"So," he said when they were seated again. "Do you have any details about anything yet? All you've told me is that you got the role. When do you start filming? How long do I have you for?"

Bella shook her head. "I don't know."

"You don't know?"

"Well, I know a few things. But not much." She shrugged. "I do know that I'll have to go——"

They were interrupted by the sharp ring of his phone .

Damn it.

Jeremy ignored it. Whoever was calling was not nearly as important as Bella.

No.

Nothing and nobody else was as important as this.

"You can get that." Bella nodded toward the phone on the coffee table.

Jeremy shook his head. "No, they'll leave a message. Ignore it."

The phone rang a few more times before it stopped.

Good. It had gone to voicemail.

"Sorry," he said apologetically. "Tell me what you know. Where do you have to——"

Again, the phone rang out, shrill, between them.

Jeremy turned, ready to shut it off completely this time. But the caller ID caught his attention.

Charlotte. She still hadn't returned his text from the night before, and although he'd been distracted all day, she'd still been on his mind.

And she never called. At least she hadn't in months and knowing what he knew...

Jeremy looked at Bella and shook his head. "I'm sorry, it's my sister. I have to get this."

Just the way he knew she would, Bella nodded and smiled. "Of course. It's not a problem. I'll get us some more crackers."

As soon as Bella stood, Jeremy snatched up the phone. "Charlotte? Is everything okay?"

"Jer?" His sister's voice was thin and shaky. "Help."

Chapter Six

"OKAY, that's the last of the boxes." Bella slammed her trunk shut and wiped her hands together before turning to look at her mother, Lisa, who'd joined them in the packing and purging the day before. Bella had been working on packing up her grandfather's house for more than a week, and could have used her mother's help a whole lot earlier, but better late than never. And her mother could do the hard work now, actually moving Roy into his new place, while she spent some more time with Jeremy.

After their day biking around town, there hadn't been much time to hang out. Not quality time, anyway. Bella had finally heard from Lewis with some of her preliminary pre-shooting schedule and it was a lot, to put it mildly. Things were about to get busy and she wanted to spend as much time as she could with Jeremy before things got crazy.

"That's it?" her mother said beside her. "Are you sure? I didn't think we'd ever finish in there."

Bella turned and crossed her arms. "*We*? What is this *we* you're talking about?" She laughed as she teased her mother. But that's all it was, teasing. She'd enjoyed the time with her grandfather as they went through his things and sorted a life-time of memories.

The Christmas ornaments he'd so lovingly collected over the years with Bella's grandmother that meant so much had been carefully packed away with the promise that one day Bella was to have them all for a tree of her own.

She'd agreed despite the fact that she didn't like to think of *one day.* But she didn't dwell on that. Instead, Bella enjoyed every moment of her grandfather's company.

Roy was full of all kinds of stories, and he'd taken immense pleasure in sharing them all in great detail with Bella as they sorted, packed, and purged. Well, as mostly *Bella* did the work while Roy *supervised.* His stories had definitely added time to the process, but Bella didn't care. She wouldn't have traded the time with Papa for anything. They'd created some more of their own memories in the little house, and she'd learned a lot about the man that she'd never known along the way.

She would never tell her, but Bella was a little disappointed that her mother had shown up because the dynamic between them had definitely changed. Lisa was much more efficient and down to business than Bella and Roy were on their own. It wasn't necessarily a bad thing that she didn't have time for the stories and memories, but Bella had enjoyed it.

"Okay, Dad," her mom said from her own car, where she'd just finished loading the items that were making the move with Roy to his new place. "Is there anything else you can think of? Anything that might be hidden in a wall, under a floorboard, in the cellar…anywhere?"

Bella looked at her mother with a question. *Why on earth would there be anything hiding in her grandfather's house?*

To her surprise, Papa shrugged casually, and then appeared to think about it before answering. "You got the files in the cubby in the back of the closet?"

Her mother nodded.

Bella's eyes widened.

"And the jewelry, behind the stove?"

Again, Bella's mother nodded confidently.

Bella looked between the two of them in wonder.

"I got those, too." Her mother crossed her arms over her chest with a grin and winked at Bella. "Dad, I know all your spots."

"I'm impressed." Papa nodded with a smile. "That should be it," he said. "If there's anything else, I guess the new owners can have it." He turned to look at his little house that he had spent decades in.

Bella gave him a moment, certain he'd be emotional. Heck, *she* was emotional. And she'd never actually lived there beyond spending summers as a teenager and then again recently.

To her surprise, her grandfather didn't seem bothered at all to leave his home. Papa nodded once at his house and turned around to face her and her mother. "Okay, let's go."

Bella stepped toward him. "Just like that? You're ready to go? You don't need to..." She wasn't sure how to finish the sentence.

Papa shook his head. "No," he said matter-of-factly. "There's nothing I need to do , Bella."

"You're not sad? Or..."

Papa put a hand on her shoulder and squeezed gently as he looked into her eyes. "Bella, it's just a house. A shell. The memories, they don't live in those walls." He pressed his mittened hand to his chest. "They live in here."

Tears came to Bella's eyes but she blinked them back before anyone noticed. "I don't really understand, Papa. You were so adamant about not moving. It took everything I had to convince you to even consider it. I just thought..."

Her grandfather smiled. "Bella, it was never about the house. And you were right all along. I shouldn't be living on my own anymore. It's time. So there's no need for me to feel anything but peace with this decision." He nodded to himself and smiled at her. "It just feels right."

Bella watched as he moved, his age slowing him more and more, to her mother's car and got in the passenger seat. Her own car was completely loaded with boxes for the donation center once again. Her mother came up beside her and put a hand on Bella's shoulder. "You've been amazing, kiddo. Thank you for helping Papa through all this."

Bella put her hand over her mother's and squeezed. "Maybe he doesn't feel anything from this house. But I can't help but feel something," she said.

"Maybe you should have kept it? You seem to really like Glacier Falls. You could have moved —"

Bella cut her off before she could get carried away. As much as she loved Glacier Falls, she couldn't keep a house. "Mom, the timing isn't right."

"That's right." She smiled. "Just as soon as I get your grandfather settled, you and I are going to have a proper catch-up. I want to hear all about what's going on in the city and this movie of yours. It's so exciting."

She gave her mom a spontaneous hug and squeezed tight.

"You're going to be a big star, Bella. I'm so proud of you, and I can't wait to hear all about it."

And Bella couldn't wait to tell her mom all about it, either. What little there still was to tell. Beyond the preliminary schedule that included meetings with trainers and voice coaches and an acting coach, she still didn't know when shooting was going to start, or where it was, or really, much of anything at all.

"I'd like that, Mom. Soon, okay? Before you go back to the city?"

Her mom squeezed her hand again. "Of course. And I want to meet this new man of yours. He sounds pretty special. I mean, he'd have to be, if you like him."

Oh, she liked him all right. Quite a bit. Bella laughed along with her mother.

"He is pretty special," Bella said with a smile. "And I really do like him. He's different."

"Oh, " her mom took a step back and assessed her daughter, "I can see that. Which is why I want to meet him. Do you think he'll be able to meet us for a drink while I'm in town? Or maybe dinner? I'd like to get to know him a little bit."

Bella nodded but she wasn't entirely sure. Something was going on with Jeremy's sister, Charlotte, and although he hadn't given Bella a ton of details about what it was exactly, she knew it was serious. Bella didn't remember the other woman from when they were growing up. Charlotte was a few years older, and had absolutely no interest in a younger girl from the city spending her summers in town. Beyond seeing her around a little bit, Bella barely knew her at all.

Everything Jeremy had ever told him about the woman she'd become had been glowing and it was clear they were good friends, which was also why Jeremy was so worried about her. Whatever it was that was going on with his sister wasn't a small thing, that much Bella knew for sure. There was no way Jeremy would be so worked up if it were a minor drama. She didn't want to push for details, especially when they weren't Jeremy's to share. But Bella knew that when the time was right, he'd let her know.

"Jeremy has a lot going on right now," Bella told her mom. "But I know he really wants to meet you, too. We'll figure out a good time."

Lisa nodded. "Sounds good to me. I'll see you at the Airbnb later? Or will you be staying with Jeremy?"

Bella blushed. It didn't matter that she was a grown adult; there were still some things that felt strange.

"I'll be there."

With Papa's house empty and ready for the new owners,

they couldn't stay there and with their relationship still pretty new, she hadn't wanted to impose on Jeremy for too long, so along with her mother, they'd rented a small cottage to use for the time being. If she was going to keep coming into town, Bella was going to have to figure out a longer term solution, but that seemed like a problem for later.

"Are we going, or not?" Papa yelled from the car, making both Bella and her mom laugh.

"You better get going," Bella said. "I think someone's excited to get to his new place." She shook her head as her mother returned to her car and pulled away from the curb. Papa didn't even look back as they drove off.

Bella stood there another minute and was just about to get in her car and make the last trip to the donation center when her phone rang.

Lewis's name and number appeared on the call display. Bella quickly pushed the button to accept the call.

"Lewis?"

"Are you sitting down?" her agent said without preamble. Bella shook her head, but didn't have a chance to tell her she wasn't, in fact, sitting down when Lewis continued, "It's been announced."

"What has?"

"The movie. The cast. *You.*"

"Me?"

Lewis laughed. "I love how completely unaware you are."

Bella shook her head and tried not to be offended.

"The studio made the official announcement on the casting," he said. "I'm going to try to have everything run through me and Michael, so—"

"Michael?"

"Your publicist."

"I have a publicist?"

"Trust me," Lewis said seriously. "You *want* a publicist.

He'll be in touch with the interview requests, but no doubt some will sneak past and try to get to you directly. If that happens, just let us know and——"

"Interviews? Get to me directly?" Bella spun around slowly, scanning the snow-covered street looking for what, or whom, she wasn't sure. But she had the sudden unsettling feeling that someone was about to pop out of a snowbank with a camera pointed at her. "What are you talking about?"

"Bella? Hang on tight," Lewis said happily. "Because you're about to go on a wild ride."

The last few days after Charlotte's phone call had been intense. The moment he'd heard his sister's voice on the line, everything else faded away. It had taken him a few minutes to calm Charlotte down enough that he could actually understand what she was saying.

When Bella returned to the living room with crackers, he shrugged an apology and mouthed, "I'm sorry."

She was so sweet and understanding. She'd kissed him on the cheek, letting her lips linger a moment before excusing herself to the bedroom so he could have some privacy. They'd finally been able to resume their date and they'd watched an old romantic comedy on the couch afterward, but he couldn't hide how distracted he'd been. He definitely couldn't tell Bella what was happening. Not until he knew for sure *what* exactly was happening. And even then, Charlotte had sworn him to secrecy. She was so embarrassed that she'd let herself get into such a situation. Besides, the last thing he wanted to burden Bella with on the night she'd gotten the best news in her life was the details of Char's situation. Jeremy felt terrible about all of it, but...he'd make it up to her.

But first, he had to help his sister.

As it had turned out, there'd been nothing Jeremy could do right then for Charlotte. She'd made the call in the middle of the night from the bathroom, when she'd been sure Billy was sleeping.

She was scared of her boyfriend, just as his dad had thought.

Scared.

His brave, strong, untouchable big sister. The very thought of some asshole laying a hand on her, making her scared in any way at all, made him see red.

He had to fight the urge to fly across the country and teach the jerk a lesson. No one messed with his sister.

"No!" Charlotte spoke firmly. It had been the first strong thing she'd said since he'd gotten her on the phone. "You can't come. It was so bad after Mom and Dad left and—"

"You don't understand." He cut her off. "I won't leave. Not without you."

That made Charlotte cry again and Jeremy silently cursed himself. He had no idea how to handle the situation. They'd had some basic training with the fire department a few years back on how to approach a domestic abuse victim, but this was different. *Very* different. This was his *sister.* And that meant all bets were off.

But Charlotte had made him promise to leave it alone. To leave Billy alone. "It will only make it worse," she pleaded. "I just want to come home."

Jeremy couldn't argue with that. If she wanted to come home, he'd make it happen. That's what brothers did. And that's what *he* would do. He just didn't know how yet.

They spoke for a few more minutes, Jeremy gathering as much information as he could from her.

They determined it would be best to contact her at the coffee shop she worked at because Billy checked her phone all the time. Jeremy had to take a deep breath at that bit of information.

What kind of man was so insecure he needed to control his girlfriend's phone?

It didn't compute. He simply could not understand the mind of a guy like that. Not that he wanted to. But by the sounds of it, he would have to try if he wanted to get Charlotte home.

"Okay," he said finally. "Let me talk to Mom and—"

"No." Charlotte's voice was laced with panic. "You can't tell them anything. I know them. They'll freak out and make everything worse."

"Char." Jeremy worked to keep his voice calm. He reached around and squeezed the back of his neck in an effort to release the tension that was quickly beginning to build there. "I have to talk to them. They already know something is up and—"

"That's the problem." She cut him off again. "Billy was not happy with their visit. He's so suspicious of them now. He won't even let me mention them. It's…just don't, okay? Can you just handle it?"

He nodded and then, even though he had no idea how, he promised her he would.

She gave him her work schedule for the next few weeks and the number for the shop.

Jeremy scribbled down the details on a pad of paper. "Okay," he said when she was done. "Don't worry, Charlotte. I'll work something out, okay? Just sit tight and I'll be in touch as soon as I can with a plan."

"Thank you, Jer."

He could sense the relief in her voice, an entire continent away, and he hoped like hell he wouldn't let her down.

He had no idea how he was going to make it happen, but without a doubt, he knew he would.

That had been two days ago, and he still didn't know how he was going to get Charlotte home. He'd tossed around a few ideas, but there was nothing definite. Short of flying to Halifax himself, picking her up and physically putting her on a plane, he couldn't think of anything that would work. Not without alerting her boyfriend that she was planning something. And from the sounds of it, she was sure he would try everything to stop her. The last thing Jeremy wanted was to make the situation worse before he could make it better.

Every day that went by, Char was in danger. A fact Jeremy was acutely aware of. He'd promised her he wouldn't tell anyone. And Jeremy was a man of his word. But he was also not a stupid man. And he knew enough to know when he needed help.

Jeremy knocked on the office door and waited.

"Come in, Davis." Ed Walker, the fire chief, called out through the shut door. The man had an uncanny sense of knowing who was there and what they needed, often before they did. It was one of the things that made him such a good chief. He'd be impossible to replace if the retirement rumors were true.

Jeremy opened the door and walked into the small office. The walls were covered in a mixture of photos of crews over the years and framed artwork from Ed's granddaughter. "How did you know it was me?" He shook his head as he took a seat across from his boss. "If I didn't know better, I'd say you have some sort of sixth sense."

"I don't know about a sixth sense." Ed laughed. "But you've been walking around for the last few days in a bit of a daze. You're clearly thinking about something. What's going on?"

Jeremy let out a breath he felt like he'd been holding since getting off the phone with Char and started to talk. "It's my sister, chief. She needs help."

Chapter Seven

"WE ARE NOW OFFICIALLY CELEBRATING!" Stephanie declared the moment Bella joined her at the table at Birchwood. She'd already called ahead and sweet-talked the owner —and most amazing chef—Brody into making them a special lunch. After all, it wasn't every day that your friend landed her very first role *and* it was in what was going to be an absolute smashing success *and* you were the co-star. No, it was not every day that happened.

Plus, now that she'd officially told Jeremy *and* the announcement had been made by the studio, they deserved to celebrate. Which was why the champagne Steph had preordered had just been delivered to the table.

Bella blushed and shook her head. "Steph, this is too much. We had drinks the other night. We don't need to—"

"Are you kidding?" She paused while the waiter popped the cork. Steph clapped a little as he poured them each two glasses. "That didn't count. And this isn't even enough." She raised a glass and waited for Bella to do the same. "We should be having a proper party. Maybe Faith and Logan can do something at Ever After. Oh, I don't know why I didn't think of that before."

Why *hadn't* she thought of that before? They deserved to have a party. And it would be such a great way to ease Bella into the spotlight. Instantly, her mind started making lists.

"I don't know." Bella interrupted her train of thought. "The timing doesn't feel right." The smile fell from Bella's face, but only momentarily.

Steph registered it as odd, but didn't say anything. Her friend had been under a lot of stress in the last little while with her grandfather. She was probably just overwhelmed.

"Well, maybe later. Maybe a huge release party?" She offered Bella a little smile before clearing her throat.

"Maybe."

"In the meantime...a cheers to you, Bella Burton. Remember this moment because it will be one of the last ones that you will go unrecognized. Soon, you will be a household name and one of the biggest stars in the entire world."

Bella shook her head and giggled. "You're ridiculous." Her smile was genuine. "But thank you." They clinked glasses and both of them drank.

Steph let the bubbles pop and dance in her mouth, enjoying the champagne the way she always did. It didn't matter how many fancy functions she'd been to, or bottles that had been poured for her—she never grew tired of the simple decadence of bubbly.

"And thank you for all of your help," Bella said a moment later. "I mean it. None of this would be happening without you, Steph. I really appreciate the way you've taken me under your wing and introduced me to Lewis and everything."

Steph couldn't help but laugh. "Sweetheart. None of this is happening because of me. Make no mistake about it. This is all you."

When Bella shook her head, Steph insisted, "Really. I may

have introduced you to Lewis, but it doesn't matter who you know if you don't have the talent to back it up. And you, my friend, have all the talent, plus some. You are ridiculously talented. I could introduce you to every single person in the industry, but if you weren't...well...*you*...this wouldn't be happening. So do not sell yourself short." Steph put her glass down, clasped her hands together, and leaned across the table. "Seriously, though. You need to own this. All of it."

"What do you mean?"

"I mean that this industry is tough. It will eat you alive if you don't have a strong sense of self, Bella. You need to believe that you deserve every single thing that will be happening to you. You earned it and you will continue to earn it. You can't doubt that, okay?"

Bella nodded. She ran her finger around the rim of her glass for a moment before looking up. "Can I ask you a question?"

"Always."

Her friend's smile was soft and shy. She bit her bottom lip, and even before she opened her mouth, Steph had a feeling she knew what she was going to ask. "How do you manage a relationship with all of this?" Bella waved her hand around the room and then laughed. "I don't mean *this*. But..."

"I know exactly what you mean." She took a moment, trying to determine exactly how honest she should be. It was no secret that Bella and Jeremy were in a new relationship. It also wasn't any secret that they both seemed to be absolutely crazy about the other. Steph wished she could tell her friend that it wasn't a problem. That her fame would allow her the flexibility to balance her social life with her professional life easily. But that would be a lie. It wasn't easy.

And it wasn't just the relationship itself that could be hard to manage. Arguably the hardest part was the attention of the press and tabloids. Or more specifically, the rumors and lies and half-truths that they liked to publish. It affected even the strongest relationship. How could it not?

Add in the crazy schedules, the unpredictable hours, long days on set, months and months apart—it was a lot.

Having a healthy, normal relationship with her career was next to impossible.

There was one time Steph thought she'd beaten the odds herself. She'd been so sure movie star Dax Combs was meant to be her destiny. And in a way, he had been. When they'd first met, she'd been completely smitten with his attentions and the fact that he didn't seem to care that she was more famous than he was. It had been a problem with men before. They were insecure or intimidated by Stephanie's level of fame. In the past, she'd dated men who'd tried to unconsciously sabotage her career, encourage her not to take roles, or try to get her to skip parties and events that they couldn't attend. But not Dax. He'd loved her fame, and he'd never seemed threatened by any of it.

Or so she'd thought.

In hindsight, Steph could see all the warning signs that things weren't exactly how they seemed. But at the time, she hadn't wanted to see any of it. Their engagement had made international news and they'd quickly become Hollywood's *it* couple. Everyone wanted to interview them, photograph them, and hire them. *Both* of them. Steph's star had risen even higher, and noticeably, so had Dax's.

The wedding was set to be a massively anticipated affair, despite the fact that Steph didn't want any of the pomp and circumstance. She would have been happy to keep it really small and intimate in a setting that took her breath away. Which was how she'd come to visit Glacier Falls and Ever After Ranch.

And even though the engagement hadn't worked out—it turned out Dax was more interested in fame than he was with her specifically—it wasn't a complete loss. Not at all. After all, if she'd never come to town, she never would have met her half-sisters or the rest of her new friends.

Things had a funny way of working out.

Too bad it wasn't that easy for romantic relationships.

But she could see that Bella didn't want to hear any of that. Instead, she smiled and told her as much of the truth as she thought she was prepared for. She shrugged and sat back in her chair. "It's hard, Bella."

"That's it?" Bella opened her eyes wide and waited. "It's *hard*?"

"It is."

Bella crossed her arms over her chest and sat back. "Come on, Steph. You're not going to give me any more advice than that?"

Of course she wanted more, but Steph wasn't going to put a damper on their celebration with any more details. Besides, she wasn't one to offer a whole lot of advice, even when it was asked for. She'd found it wasn't always well received, and she liked Bella. She didn't want to mess up their friendship by being too honest. But she would give her something. "Okay," Steph said after a moment. "I'll say one more thing, but that's it, okay?"

Bella nodded, listening.

"It's important for you to remember that this is your life and this is an incredible opportunity for you. It will change your life in so many ways that you don't even fully understand yet. There will be time for everything, but right now, what is happening...enjoy it, okay? Be in the moment and don't let anyone try to tell you different. You won't get this moment back, so try to have no distractions. Okay?"

Bella stared at her for a moment, unspeaking. Finally, she swallowed and nodded slowly. Steph had just given her a non-answer and they both knew it.

With the final decisions made about casting for *Bombshell* and the official announcement made, Stephanie knew things were about to start moving quickly and production would be ramping up before she knew it, which was why she needed to take care of a few things in Glacier Falls before life got too crazy again.

After their celebratory lunch, where Steph had tried to shift the conversation away from relationships and how hard they were, and into the safer territory about Bella's grandfather's move, and then the much more fun territory of what Bella could expect with the ambitious filming schedule that she was sure would be rolling out, Steph shifted gears into her new project. Which was equally, if not more, exciting for her than a new movie.

She had so many plans for the Lynx Creek cabins and the old fishing camp and what it could become, but she lacked one very important thing—experience. Okay, she lacked two things —experience and time. Which was why she hoped her sisters and their husbands could help her out and come through on a project manager she could hire to oversee everything.

The kitchen at the Turner sisters' house was the hub of almost all of the family activity. Which was a lot…and about to become even busier when the baby was born, which meant Steph really should find a new place to live. Soon.

With Hope on bed rest because of her high-risk pregnancy, the doctor had okayed small bits of walking from her bed as long as she sat down most of the time, so they'd moved a large recliner into the corner of the kitchen so she could join in all the family conversations and activity. It was an arrangement that made Hope happy because she was going crazy sitting alone upstairs, but not all of the other family members were quite as pleased with the move.

Hope had a tendency to be a bit of a control freak when it came to their wedding business. Although she'd had no problem relinquishing control when she and Levi were traveling the world on their honeymoon, things were very different now that she was home with nothing to do. Faith was trying to be patient, but everyone could see the toll it was taking on her. After all, she hadn't even wanted to run the wedding business in the first place. Of course, now that she had, she was happy for her sister to butt out. Or at least for her sister to work *with* her instead of bossing her around from the chair in the corner.

It wasn't a secret that Faith was desperate for the baby to be born so her twin sister would have a distraction and leave her to it. Until then, any distraction was welcome.

Just as Steph had predicted, Hope was set up in her chair in the corner of the kitchen when she got there, and Faith was nowhere to be found. Hope had a pot of tea on the table next to her, and a laptop balanced on her swollen stomach. She looked up with a grin when Steph walked in.

"I'm so glad you're back."

"You are?" She gave her sister a kiss on the cheek. "Where's everyone else?"

Hope pressed her lips together and shook her head. "They're out in the barn, getting set up for a wedding this weekend, and they refused to take me. I tried to show them this new thing with the napkins, and I found the cutest idea for a winter photo background that would be absolutely perfect on the far side of the barn, but they wouldn't listen to me. I told them I could show them really quickly. But they said something about the wheelchair and snow and left."

"Good," Steph answered quickly, trying not to laugh. "You're not supposed to overdo it, Hope, and you know it."

Her response didn't seem to satisfy her sister, who dismissed her with a wave. "I'm not overdoing anything if I'm sitting in my chair."

"Besides, I thought you were doing a family tree on the genealogy site or something?" Steph hadn't really wanted to ask about that particular project because she knew that part of Hope's idea to research the family tree also had to do with finding out who exactly Stephanie's father was. Their mother had fallen pregnant before she married the twins' father, and had given her up for adoption. Faith had overheard her parents fighting about it when she was a young girl. She'd lived with the secret up until recently, and even through their parents' tragic death years earlier, but had finally come clean to Hope about what she knew. They put the pieces of the puzzle together to discover that Stephanie was actually their mother's daughter who she'd given up for adoption. But they still didn't know any details about who her birth father was. Although there was definitely part of Steph that wanted to know, there was also a large part of her that didn't.

Now, Hope looked at her cautiously, obviously trying to gauge how much she wanted to know. "I haven't really gotten very far with that lately," she said after a moment. "Did you want me to—"

"No, that's fine," she said quickly. "Tell me how you're feeling."

Hope's face shifted away from concern as her hands rubbed over her belly. "Huge." She laughed.

They spent the next few minutes chatting about the baby and Hope's health. She'd been diagnosed with uterine cancer but had postponed treatment for the pregnancy. Which was part of what made everything high risk, and was completely why everyone was concerned about her. As soon as the baby was born, not only would Hope have her hands full with a newborn, she'd also start with her treatment and potentially surgery as soon as possible.

After a few minutes of catch-up, Steph looked at the clock over the stove. "I'd love to keep chatting, Hope. But

I'm actually supposed to have a meeting this afternoon." She gave her sister a guilty look and shrugged casually. "I need help with my Lynx Creek project, especially now that I've taken on a new movie project and I don't know the first thing about where to start. Levi and Logan were going to introduce me to a man named Travis something. He used to be a—"

"Ranch hand at the Langdon ranch," Hope finished for her and Steph nodded. "Travis is great. And so much more than just a ranch hand. He's kind of one of those guys who's just really good at everything, if you know what I mean."

Did she know what Hope meant? She'd said it innocently enough, but Steph couldn't help but think there was a hidden meaning there. She shook her head clear and focused on the rest of what she was saying.

"I know they hated to let him go when Debbie sold the ranch, and we just don't have enough work around here for him. He's really a great guy. Are you sure they weren't trying to set you up?"

"What?" So she hadn't been imagining it. There was definitely something underlying Hope's description of the man, but Steph did not have the time or patience for a setup of any kind. Even by her super bored pregnant sister. She shook her head. "No. There is no way. I told them I was looking for someone to—"

"Ohh, I see."

"You don't see anything." Steph shook her head. She knew Hope was desperate for something to do, but inventing a setup situation was too far. "I need a contractor, not a—"

"Date."

"What?" Steph shook her head. "It's not a—"

"Date? Damn, is this a blind date?"

Startled by the deep voice behind her, Steph spun around on her heel to look into the eyes of the sexiest cowboy she'd ever seen. Hell, the sexiest cowboy or not that she'd seen in a very long time.

His dark eyes flashed with humor as he took his hat off and ran a hand through his thick hair. "I would have dressed a little more, well…a bit more date appropriate."

Steph thought he looked just fine to her. His well-worn jeans hugged thick, strong leg muscles. He wore a thick wool coat, but she could imagine the hard chest and equally strong arms that were hiding under it. Muscles defined from working outside in the elements. *Damn.*

"Steph?"

She blinked hard out of the trance she'd been in and looked to Hope, who wasn't even trying to hide the grin on her face.

"Meet Travis. Travis, meet Steph."

Regaining control of herself, Steph extended a hand to the man. "Travis. It's nice to meet you. And no, it's not a date."

His cocky grin didn't falter as his large hand wrapped around hers, completely unaware of the fire he'd ignited deep inside her, and winked. "Well, that's a shame."

Isn't it ever.

The heat lingered on her skin when he removed his hand from hers. Steph followed it back to his front pocket, where he casually slid it.

It took her a moment to catch herself and realize she was staring at the man. When Hope giggled behind her, she shook her head and pasted a confident smile on her face. "Maybe we should go somewhere and talk," she said. And then, realizing the way it sounded, Steph quickly added, "About my project, I mean."

"Of course." His smile was slow. He took a breath and exhaled slowly, his eyes never leaving hers.

Steph needed to look away before she said something stupid. Again.

"Okay, great." She focused on her notebook and the stack of papers she had. "Why don't we go to…" *Where were they going to go?* Her plan had been to meet the man at Ever After. She never intended to go anywhere with him. And now that she knew how dangerously sexy he was…being alone with him was probably a bad idea.

No. It was a very bad idea. Because if what Logan and Levi told her about Travis was true, he was a hell of a good contractor and he was exactly what she needed to whip her camp into shape while she was busy on set. She couldn't afford to mess that up by getting involved with him.

No matter how badly she might want to all of a sudden.

Steph turned around, her mind made up, and pressed her lips together. "On second thought, I think we could probably just have our little meeting in the living room."

Chapter Eight

BELLA TOOK a few extra minutes in the mirror, getting ready. She was nervous, but excited too. Jeremy was going to meet her mom over dinner. And although she was a grown woman, who made her own decisions, she still couldn't help but hope that the meeting would go well. Not that she had any reason to believe it wouldn't, but still...Bella hadn't introduced a man to her parents since...well, since she was a senior in high school and that was only because he'd picked her up to take her to prom.

This was different.

Really different.

She cared about Jeremy. And her mother's support meant a lot to her. Especially because Bella knew it wasn't going to be easy balancing a new relationship with her soon-to-be very busy schedule. She hadn't even really had a chance to discuss it with Jeremy because he'd been so busy with work and with the drama going on with his sister.

But it wasn't Bella's style to worry about things until there was something to worry about. Besides, after dinner, they'd be able to have that heartfelt talk and sort it all out. Because she only had a few days before she was going to have to leave again. As for her mother, Lisa was heading back home the next day. So if there was going to be a meet-the-parents moment, it was now or never.

Steph's voice echoed in her memory. "It's hard. No distractions."

Bella refused to think that Steph was right about this. Maybe she'd just been dating the wrong type of men? She wasn't Stephanie, and Jeremy was different. And he cared about her. She knew he did. He wanted her to be successful. Jeremy knew how much her career meant to her, and he also knew what that meant. No, it didn't matter what Steph said about relationships. Jeremy was different. *She* and Jeremy were different. They'd make it work. She believed that.

She had to.

"I'm so excited to meet him," her mom said as Bella joined her in the kitchen, where Lisa was reheating the dishes they picked up from Birchwood earlier in the day. They'd decided to host Jeremy at their Airbnb instead of going out. But once they made that decision, mother and daughter both realized neither of them actually wanted to cook anything.

"I sure hope you like him." Bella grabbed a dish and began to scoop the vegetables out of the box and into it before covering it in foil and popping it in the oven to warm. "But of course, I know you will."

"I'm sure I will." Her mother's smile was friendly. "You just seem so different when you talk about him. Not at all like that last guy. What was his name again?"

"Kyle." Bella rolled her eyes. She didn't like thinking about that part of her life, let alone talking about it. It hadn't been all that long ago when she'd on-again/off-again dated her band-leader at the time. He'd promised her fame and record deals. But mostly what he gave her was heartache, cheating, and general douche baggery.

Jeremy was different in almost every way. Definitely in all the ways that mattered.

"Mom, Jeremy is nothing like Kyle. He was just a...a mistake of the most epic proportions. But that being said, if I hadn't ever known Kyle and then finally gotten fed up enough with his cheating to quit the band that last time, I probably never would have come to Glacier Falls for Christmas. In fact, I probably wouldn't be here right now and I never would have met Jeremy, or Steph, and none of this would be happening to me right now."

Bella let herself think about that for a minute and really soak it in. It was true. Everything really did happen for a reason, and, as much of a pain in the ass that he'd been, her time with Kyle had definitely led her to exactly where she was right now. Still, she thought with a grin, it didn't mean she was going to be grateful for him in any way.

She laughed at herself and went back to getting dinner ready.

"And what does Jeremy think about the movie?" Her mom asked the question Bella knew she would. "He must be very excited for you."

Bella nodded but didn't make eye contact. "He is." It wasn't a lie. Jeremy was excited for her.

"And?" her mother continued. "What does he think about that shooting schedule you were telling me about? It sure seems like a lot."

Bella swallowed hard. She may not have had a chance to tell Jeremy about the upcoming schedule. But she *had* told her mom.

"Well, he's good with it." It wasn't really a lie. After all, Bella was absolutely sure that Jeremy would be good with it. Or at least she *hoped* he would be good with it when she finally had a chance to discuss it with him. And hope was almost as good as certainty in this particular situation.

"He is?" Lisa didn't bother trying to hide her surprise. "Wow. He really must be a special kind of man because I don't think I know many guys who'd be happy about being away from their new girlfriend for so long at the beginning of a relationship. What is it, three months?"

Bella bit her bottom lip. "Four. But that's after three weeks of the preliminary stuff in the city."

Her mom opened her eyes wide but thankfully didn't say a word. Especially because Jeremy chose that moment to knock on the door.

"Dinner was delicious, Lisa. Thank you." Jeremy wiped his mouth and dropped his napkin to the plate in front of him. "In fact, that beef tenderloin was almost as good as the one I had at Birchwood last time I was there."

Next to him, Bella snickered. Jeremy put his hand on her leg under the table and squeezed. She'd let him in on the secret that they'd ordered in food from the restaurant, but when Lisa didn't offer up the information, he'd made the decision to play with her a little bit.

"It's funny you say that, Jeremy." Lisa stood to gather the plates. "Because as I'm sure my lovely daughter has already told you, I'm not much of a cook."

Bella burst out laughing. "Sorry, Mom. I couldn't help it."

Lisa rolled her eyes. "Right. Well, I did you a favor by bringing in takeout, Jeremy. I assure you." She paused and looked him in the eye, a friendly smile on her face.

He nodded with a chuckle as he pushed back from his own chair. "Well, even if you didn't cook it, Lisa, you have amazing taste when it comes to selecting takeout."

"That I do." She winked at him.

"Please." Jeremy took the plates from her hand. "Let me clear up. It's the least I can do."

She released the dishes to him and sat down. It had been awhile since Jeremy had to try to win over the parents of a girlfriend, and he'd been nervous. Especially because Bella meant more to him than any other girlfriend he'd had in the past. But he needn't have been worried. Lisa had been gracious and welcoming and just as open and friendly as her daughter.

"Let me." Bella stood next to him. "You sit and get to know each other a bit more." Bella smoothly took the stack of plates from his hands. "I'll clear up." She winked at him. "Have some wine. You deserve it after the week you've had."

He couldn't argue with that. It *had* been a lot. Jeremy reached for the bottle, topped up Lisa's glass and then his own. "I can definitely drink to that."

"Bella told me it's been very stressful for you lately," Lisa said kindly. "Concern for a family member can be quite difficult."

He nodded, not wanting to get into details, but also not wanting to be rude. Lisa seemed to understand his need for privacy on the matter and she smoothly changed the topic. They'd kept the conversation light through dinner, focused mostly on his job, and Bella growing up, and what Lisa and her husband did to keep busy in the city—nothing too deep. Jeremy had been waiting for Lisa to put the gears to him a little bit, and he wasn't disappointed.

"You seem to be quite smitten with my daughter." Her smile was warm, but Jeremy could see the caution in her eyes.

Of course she'd be concerned. She was a mother and that's what mothers did. They were concerned for their children.

It was Jeremy's job to put her mind at ease as much as he could. "I really care about Bella," he said seriously. "She is..."

He shook his head in wonder, the way he often did when he thought about her. "She's special."

"That she is." Lisa sat back in her chair and smiled to herself. "And it sounds like the whole world is going to know it soon as well. Her father and I are very proud of her." She chuckled a little. "And don't even get me started about her grandfather. Her papa is incredibly proud of her, too."

"Is he ever!" Jeremy laughed. "And with good reason, too. You all have so much to be proud of. Bella is incredibly talented. The moment I heard her sing, I knew her talent was special. And you're right—the rest of the world will know that soon enough, too. It's all really exciting for her and so well deserved."

Lisa sipped at her wine but never took her eyes off him. Her laughter had died and her gaze turned serious. "And how do you feel about it all, Jeremy? About how busy she's going to be right away here? Her schedule sure sounds intense. It's going to be quite a challenge for the two of you and a new relationship, I'm sure."

Something about the way she asked the question set alarms off in Jeremy's head. Of course Bella was going to be busy working. He didn't expect anything else. After all, it took time to make a movie. And a movie that she was not only acting in, but also singing on almost every track? That also meant recording an entire album. It was definitely going to be a busy time, and although Bella hadn't told him any of the details of her schedule yet, he wasn't completely naive to what being the star meant. "I'm sure it will be a lot," he said after a moment. "How could it not be, right?"

Lisa nodded slowly, but didn't speak.

"And we'll make it work," Jeremy continued. "Because that's the only choice we have."

She didn't speak for another moment, but finally, Lisa

leaned forward and placed her wineglass down carefully. "Is it?" she asked. "The *only* choice?"

Jeremy shook his head and sat back. "I'm afraid I don't understand what you're saying." In truth, he was afraid that he knew *exactly* what she was saying. And he didn't like it. Not even a little bit.

"I'm just saying, with Bella's career taking off now, what does that look like for you? You're not the type of man to get jealous, are you? Or the smothering type? I mean, she will be gone for long periods and—"

"I assure you, Mrs. Burton," the moment called for the use of her formal name, "that I only want what's best for Bella, too. I know that we're still new, but I have full faith that our relationship can survive all kinds of obstacles and bumps in the road."

She bit her bottom lip and nodded slowly. In that moment, she looked so much like her daughter, it was startling. "I understand and I appreciate that, Jeremy. I do. But I think it's important to know the difference between *bumps* in the road, and the road itself. Relationships are hard. I can't even imagine the extra challenge there would be to have a partner who was on the road to fame. The world is about to open up to her. A whole world and everyone in it, too."

He let her words settle over him as his brain worked to formulate a response. But before he could add to the conversation, she'd once again changed the topic.

"Tell me," Lisa said, her kind smile back in place. "Have you always wanted to be a firefighter?"

The change in topic was abrupt, but not unwelcome. Jeremy loved to talk about his job, and he was more than happy not to dwell on the idea that their relationship was in trouble before it even got going. He pushed the flicker of worry she'd sparked in him aside and focused on the moment. "Since I was a little boy," he said with a smile. "It sounds silly, but when I was six years old, my sister and I had a cat. Mittens." He smiled to himself at the memory of his one and only cat. "One day, she was chased up a tree by the neighbor's dog and even though my mom and dad insisted she'd come down on her own, she didn't. Not for two days. Every day, I went outside and called her. I opened cans of tuna and everything. Still, she was terrified. And I was devastated. Every day that she didn't come down from that tree, I'd sit at the base of it and cry."

Lisa's hand fluttered to her chest. "That's terrible."

"It was," he agreed. "Very traumatic for a little boy." He winked and she laughed. "And then one day a firetruck drove up the street toward my house. The lights were flashing and everything, so it got everyone's attention. The truck stopped in front of the house and a firefighter named Ed Walker stepped out. He walked right over to me, crouched down, and promised me that he'd get my cat safely out of the tree if I could hold his helmet for him."

"Is that right?"

Jeremy nodded. It was all a very true story. He could still remember the moment as if it had happened yesterday. "Honestly," he continued, "I didn't believe it myself, but right in front of me, they extended the ladder and Ed Walker himself climbed up to get Mittens as I clutched that heavy helmet as tightly as I could. I had convinced myself that if I let it drop, he wouldn't be able to save my cat."

"And did he? Save Mittens?" Lisa leaned forward, her elbows on the table now, waiting to hear how the story would end. "Was she okay?"

"She was fine. Lived to be almost twenty." Jeremy laughed. "Crazy old for a cat. Ed Walker, on the other hand...he suffered a few scratches. One that scarred. But he kept his promise and handed me my cat when I handed him back his helmet."

"And ever since then..."

Jeremy nodded. "I know it seems kind of crazy. It wasn't a burning building, or a grand rescue. It was a cat. But there was something about that firefighter. He inspired a six-year-old boy that day."

"And that firefighter is the chief now." Bella rejoined them. She put her hand on his shoulder and squeezed. "And rumor has it that that little six-year-old boy is next in line for the chief job when Ed retires soon."

It filled his heart with pride to hear Bella say that. He put his own hand over hers and smiled at her. "That's the rumor, but I don't want to get ahead of myself. Nothing is official until it's official."

He turned back toward Lisa, who also looked suitably impressed. But there was something else in the woman's expression. Something he couldn't completely make out. But it relit that flicker of worry in his gut. A flicker that sparked into a full flame of worry when Lisa nodded and casually said, "Well, it sure looks like both of you have some very exciting career changes in store. It should be an interesting year."

Chapter Nine

"WELL?"

Bella handed her mom a cup of tea and sat next to her on the couch. She pulled her legs up under her and rested her arm on the cushion, waiting for her mom to tell her what she thought of Jeremy. Not that she was worried. The evening had gone perfectly. The conversation had flowed and from what Bella could tell, they'd gotten along really well.

She'd been hoping to leave with Jeremy after dinner so they could finally have some time alone, but he'd been called into the station to cover for a few hours. They'd said goodnight with a long kiss. Jeremy said he had a surprise for her before she had to go back to the city. He'd kissed her long and hard and left her with the promise of a romantic and special day together.

And although it wasn't exactly what she'd been hoping for, the evening with her mother did give Bella a chance to get her feedback.

"He's very nice." Lisa blew on her tea but didn't look up.

"Nice?"

"He is."

Bella sat up straight and put her own cup down on the table. "I agree, but I feel like there's more you want to say."

She waited, but her mom still didn't elaborate. With a dramatic sigh, Bella hugged her knees. "Is that all you have to say, Mom? Really? He's nice. That's it?"

Her mom took a small, tentative sip of the tea before squeezing her eyes shut for a moment. When she opened them again, she looked right at her daughter. "I'm not sure what else you'd like me to say, Bella. Jeremy really is a nice man. He has a great life here in Glacier Falls and a career that, by the sounds of it, is about to get even better here shortly."

Bella nodded. There was something her mother wasn't saying, and she was pretty sure she knew what it was.

"And?"

"And..." Lisa drew out the word. "And I think that if the situation was different, he'd be absolutely perfect for you."

Something deep in Bella's gut twisted. "The situation?"

Her mother's smile was kind but Bella knew her mother well. She wasn't going to sugarcoat anything.

"Bella, your entire life is about to change. If none of that was happening, and you were content to settle down and live a quiet, simple life in Glacier Falls, then yes, I think he's perfect for you. But that's not what's about to happen." She took a deep breath. "You're about to be a big star. And you're going to have to spend long periods of time away from Glacier Falls. You can't be a huge star and live in a tiny mountain town in the middle of nowhere. You know that."

She nodded. She *did* know that.

"And he doesn't seem like the kind of man who'd drop his whole life here to follow a woman. Even one as amazing as you."

"I wouldn't want him to."

"I know, sweetheart." She put her tea down next to Bella's and scooted closer to her on the couch. "I know you'd never want a man like that. There's a reason you've fallen for Jeremy. He's a strong man, with his own life. And that's important."

Bella nodded numbly. It *was* important. She'd finally found a good man who had values and morals and a full life of his own. *And...why did that all of a sudden seem like a bad thing?*

"But," her mom continued, "I need you to really think about it, Bella. Does a relationship really have a chance with that much distance? With this kind of life you're about to embark on?"

"We can make it work." Even as she spoke the words, they fell flat to Bella's own ears. *Could they? Could they really beat the odds and make it work?*

She inhaled deeply, letting the air fill her lungs. Did she believe her own declaration? She wanted to. More than anything, she wanted to believe that they could make it work. No matter what. But the truth was...she didn't know.

She knew what she hoped, but Bella also wasn't naive. Hope wasn't enough.

The truth was, she'd never planned for any of this. Not for Jeremy. Not for a movie deal. None of it.

And if she had to choose...she shook her head.

She couldn't. She wouldn't choose. Because she was afraid to admit what that choice might actually be.

Besides, she reasoned with herself, no one was asking her to.

Not yet.

She forced a smile. "I don't think there's anything to worry about. Jeremy's really excited for me."

"There's a difference between being excited about the *idea* of something and living the reality."

Dammit, she hated it when her mom was right.

"I'm your mother, Bella, and I worry. And Jeremy does seem like a really nice man. I just want to make sure you're being fair."

"Fair?"

"To both of you."

Fair.

What wasn't fair was that her mom was making her question things she didn't want to question, when she should only be celebrating. She dropped her chin to her chest.

"Bella." Her mom's voice was soft when she spoke again. "I know the timing isn't perfect with Jeremy, and I know you don't want to hear this, but—"

"Don't say it." Bella groaned. "I really don't think I can hear it right now."

"I was just going to say that if it's meant to be, it'll all work out."

She groaned again and grabbed a cushion from the couch to bury her face in. "Mom, really. If you have to give me non-advice, do you think you could at least make it a little less cliche?"

Bella forced a laugh, and Lisa smiled. The mood lightened a little.

Her mom reached for her hand and squeezed. "Seriously, kiddo. I'm really proud of you." Her mother's eyes shone with unshed tears.

"Thanks, Mom. I know you—"

"No." The tear slipped down her cheek. "I mean it. And I want you to know that. I know there'll be some challenges ahead for you. But whatever you do, don't let those challenges derail you from this path. This is what you were meant to do. I believe that."

Bella giggled so she wouldn't cry. "You sound like Papa."

"Well, he's a pretty smart man." Lisa squeezed her hand in her own. "I mean it, Bella. I like Jeremy, I do. But as your mother, I need to make sure you understand that when it comes to your dreams, don't let anything or anyone stand in your way, okay? There will always be some part of you wondering *what if*. I meant it when I said that it would find a way if it was meant to be. Cliche or not," she added quickly as she swiped at her eyes.

She promised she wouldn't let anything stand in the way of what she really wanted. But long after Bella had gone to bed for the night, she lay awake, a question replaying over and over in her head. *What was it that she really wanted?*

"You know things like this are exactly why you're going to get the chief job, don't you?"

Natalie Collins, the rookie on Jeremy's crew, tossed him a can of soda.

"Thanks." Jeremy cracked the can. He needed the caffeine. "What do you mean? Things like what?"

Natalie flopped down on the couch across from him. "Things like cancelling your plans to come in because Jessie had to go home sick." Natalie took a deep drink of her soda. "Not everyone would do it."

"What are you talking about? Of course everyone would do it. If Jessie's sick, he's sick. We can't have him here throwing up all over the station. And it's not like it's an optional job. It's our duty to serve."

Natalie pointed at him with her drink. "That right there. That's why you're totally going to be the chief."

Jeremy shook his head with a chuckle. It's not that he totally disagreed with the woman. He did think he had a great shot at getting the chief job, particularly because Ed Walker himself had hinted at it. But he disagreed with her that it was because he cared more than everyone else. All of his colleagues cared the same amount. *Didn't they?* He shrugged and took another deep pull of his drink. "Nothing has been announced yet," he said. "And we don't even know for sure that Ed is retiring."

Natalie raised her eyebrows and he laughed.

"Still," he added. "I'm not going to get excited about anything until there's something concrete."

What he didn't tell Natalie was that less than thirty minutes ago, he actually did have something concrete. Well, more concrete than he had before. Jeremy hadn't expected to see the chief at the station when he'd come in, but the older man had been at his desk when he'd arrived. He'd looked preoccupied, so beyond offering him a wave as he walked by, Jeremy wasn't going to interrupt him. But almost as if Ed had been waiting for him, he waved him into the room the moment he saw him.

"I'm glad you're here."

"No problem," he said casually. "Doesn't sound like Jessie's in a good way and—"

"I don't mean that." Ed interrupted him. "But that's good too." He looked as though he were going to say something else, but changed tacks. "In fact, it's really good, Jeremy. I can always count on you. Everyone can."

Jeremy nodded.

"It's no secret, I'm winding down and—"

"No one is rushing you out the door, Chief. You have as much time as—"

He cut him off with a wave of his hand and a chuckle. "Truth is, I'm done and everyone knows it. I'm ready to spend my days fishing and watching my granddaughter grow up. I haven't announced it yet, Jeremy, so keep it quiet for now, but I'll be retiring in the spring. And unless you don't want it, I can't think of anyone better to replace me."

The last thing Jeremy had expected when he picked up the shift was to hear such a proclamation, and even though it was everything he'd been hoping to hear, he was caught off guard.

He sat back in his chair and inhaled deeply, sucking the air in through his nose before releasing it with a grin. "Wow, I..."

"Don't want it?"

"Hell yes, I want it." He all but hollered, catching himself at the last moment to keep his voice in check. "Yes," he said again, calmer. "I want it. It would be an honor, sir. Really, I..." He shook his head, unable to find the words.

"I know that's not what you expected when you came in here tonight."

"To put it mildly."

Ed chuckled. "Honestly, I didn't expect to spring it on you either. In fact, that's not what I wanted to talk about right now."

Jeremy caught the edge of seriousness in his voice, and sat up as the chief shifted gears.

"I got in touch with a fire hall in Halifax, down the street from your sister's coffee shop. They're going to help us out."

All of Jeremy's nerve endings cracked to life at the mention of his sister. It had only been a few days since he'd discussed the problem with Ed, but he'd promised to help as much as he could and Jeremy had trusted that. Even so, he hadn't been able to stop worrying about his sister in such a situation.

"If there's anything she needs to bring with her, keeping in mind it shouldn't be much, she can bring it to the coffee shop on her shift. Joe Black is the chief out there. He's going to make a point and check in on her every time she's working. He'll hang onto her belongings, if she has any she wants to bring with her, and then we'll have a plane ticket ready for her next week. The plan will be for her to go to work as normal."

Jeremy nodded. So far, it was a good plan.

"Good. Because Billy checks on her."

Ed nodded. Jeremy had filled him in on all the details about the controlling asshole of a boyfriend. "Two hours into her shift, she'll go on break and walk down the street to the fire hall. Joe will personally take her to the airport and stand guard until the plane takes off. Where you'll be waiting to pick her up. Safe."

Jeremy exhaled and felt some of the stress he'd been holding leave his body. But only some. He still needed his sister home safe.

"I'll call her and—"

"No." Ed cut him off. "With everything you've told me, we did a little more digging and Joe had his buddy on the force look into this guy. Everyone agrees it's best to move slowly and not give him any idea that Charlotte is planning to leave."

Jeremy nodded.

"So it's probably best if you let Joe communicate with her casually at the coffee shop. He'll order a dark roast and let her know she can trust him. Is there something that only she would know that will help?"

Jeremy instantly didn't like the idea of being cut out of the *rescue mission*. Char was *his* sister. She'd asked *him* for help. But he wasn't so hardheaded that he couldn't see the need to be discreet. Billy might get suspicious if all of a sudden he was calling more. Logically, he knew it was for the best. Still...

"Tell her that he's a friend of Mittens'."

Ed tipped his head, his lips twitching up in a smile. "Mittens? Is that..."

Jeremy nodded. "She'll remember." He dropped his head and breathed in deeply. "Thank you," he said when he looked up. "You have no idea what this means to me."

The older man sat back in his chair and nodded once. "I do know. And I know you'd do the same."

After leaving the chief's office, Jeremy splashed water on his face before returning to the lounge and the others. There was so much he couldn't tell his crew about. He also couldn't let them see anything was going on. That was part of being a good leader.

Which apparently was what he would be.

Brought back into the present, he looked over at Natalie, who watched him strangely.

"You good, Davis?"

He nodded and laughed before taking a deep drink of his soda. "Never been better."

"I bet." Jason O'Neil, another of his crew, and one of the guys Jeremy was closest with, chose that moment to walk in. "Bella's back in town."

"Ohh yes," Natalie chimed in. "You're so quiet about her."

"I am not."

He wasn't; they just hadn't asked.

"We have a few minutes now," Natalie said. Jason plopped in the couch next to her and crossed his arms. "Tell me everything. I heard she's going to be doing a movie with Stephanie Starz. That's crazy."

"How did you know?"

"Everyone knows."

"It's true." Jason nodded in agreement. "Everyone knows."

Natalie pushed up from the couch and stretched her arms over her head with a groan. "I can't sit anymore." She folded herself in half and wrapped her arms around the backs of her legs, completely oblivious to the man sitting behind her, whose eyes had opened wide. Jason was clearly both trying to watch Natalie, and at the same time, trying *not* to watch her because it might be considered inappropriate.

He looked to Jeremy in help, but Jeremy just shrugged and tried not to smile. He'd seen the way Jason looked at Natalie. He was interested in her, that much was clear. At least to Jeremy. But he was pretty sure it wasn't fully clear to either Natalie or even Jason, who, as far as Jeremy could tell, didn't have much confidence with women.

"It's a small town," Natalie said, her voice muffled from her position. Her arms whipped up quickly and landed on the floor in front of her as her legs jumped back into a pike. "I mean, I barely even know anyone and I heard about it." Natalie had moved into town and taken the job as the rookie at the station a few months earlier.

He hadn't considered that she might not know many people. Jeremy felt a twinge of guilt that he'd been so distracted with Bella that he hadn't thought to introduce Natalie to anyone.

The idea caught him off guard and made him chuckle. Maybe he did care more than the others.

"Rumor has it that she'll be in LA for months." Natalie moved through a sequence of poses and moves while both Jason and Jeremy watched in wonder.

"What are you doing?" Jason asked. "That is the craziest thing I've ever seen."

From the inverted position she held, Natalie tilted her head and peered out at him. "You've never seen yoga before?"

"Of course I've seen yoga before."

Jason shook his head and looked to Jeremy, who offered, "Bella does it, too. But it's totally different. She mostly sits on the floor and stretches. This is…"

"It's definitely a more active type of yoga," Natalie said from an upside down position. "It gets my blood moving so I don't fall asleep. Bella probably does more of a gentle practice."

"I don't know what she's practicing for," Jeremy said with wonder. "But the two of you are both very…bendy."

She laughed and contoured her body into a different position. "You guys should try it."

"I don't think so." Jason shook his head and settled back on the couch.

Maybe Jason didn't want to try it himself, but Jeremy couldn't help but think he didn't mind watching it at all.

"What about you, Jer? It's good for stress. You might like it."

"Stress?" Jeremy put his drink down and crossed his arms up behind his head. "What makes you think I'm stressed?"

Natalie pulled herself up into a lunge and pointed her arms out in either direction before answering him. "Well, I couldn't help but notice that you didn't comment when I mentioned Bella's movie and that she'd be gone for a long time." She shrugged a little and bent her knee deeper into a lunge. "I just assumed that would be a little stressful. I mean, I've never had a boyfriend but I can imagine that if I did, it would suck to be apart for so long and—"

"Wait." He sat up, dropped his elbows to his knees and stared at her. Jeremy couldn't help but notice that he wasn't the only one who'd picked up on the comment. Across the room, Jason was trying not to look interested. "You've never had a boyfriend?" He was aware that her personal life was really none of his business, and she hadn't really offered up many details, but despite the fact that it was nosy and he really had no business prying too much, he'd much rather steer the conversation away from his own life.

She grinned. "We're not talking about me right now."

"We could be."

She shook her head and changed the subject back. "So?" she asked. "Are you? Stressed, I mean. About Bella being away so much."

Clearly, she was not going to drop the subject. The truth was, Jeremy hadn't been stressed about it at all. Probably because he'd had so much else on his mind that he hadn't had time to think about what it would mean when she left. In fact, they hadn't even had time to talk about her schedule. So, no, he hadn't been stressed. Key word, *hadn't* been stressed at all. That was, until Lisa mentioned it to him earlier. No, she hadn't *mentioned* it so much as *warned* him about her daughter's busy schedule and what that was going to mean.

Yes. It had definitely been a warning.

"Hello?" Natalie had broken her pose and waved a hand in front of his face. "Where did you go there?"

He forced a grin. "I was just thinking." Jeremy shook his head. He was not about to tell her that her comment had sparked concern in him. Major concern. What *would* it mean when Bella started working? When would they see each other? Would they be able to find time for each other? Would he be okay with the distance? One simple comment had opened the gates of more questions than he had answers for, and the last thing he needed to do was explain any of that to Natalie.

He scrubbed a hand over his face and finished the rest of the soda in his can before wiggling his eyebrows and shifting the conversation to safer ground. "So why haven't you had a boyfriend before? No one worthy of the job?"

Chapter Ten

THE NEXT MORNING, Bella woke up with a headache throbbing just behind her left eye. She would have preferred to roll over and go back to sleep, but she had a date with Jeremy. Normally that would have been enough to get her up and out of bed, but she couldn't seem to shake the feeling of worry that had settled over her at some point in the night. She'd tossed and turned for hours, thinking about what her mother had said about Jeremy.

He had a life in Glacier Falls. A good life. A life that had a lot of opportunity for him. After all, he was going to get the fire chief job. He'd be settled for life.

But Bella's future was anywhere but Glacier Falls. Everyone knew that. Sure, Stephanie spent lots of time in the small town, but that's only because she was already a star. She'd hit a completely different level of fame than Bella could even dream of reaching one day. The level where you set your own schedule and could live wherever you wanted because everyone would come to you and work around your needs and wants. That wasn't normal and Bella knew it.

She might not know much about the industry yet, but she

knew enough to know she had to pay her dues. She had to be where things were happening and decisions were being made. And that was *not* Glacier Falls.

Something would have to give. She just hoped like hell it wasn't her brand-new relationship.

She let the hot, steamy water of the shower wash her concerns down the drain as she came to a decision. Maybe there was something to worry about when it came to her and Jeremy, but maybe there wasn't. What she did know was that it would make her crazy to keep obsessing about it. And that's the last thing she needed because Steph was right: *Bombshell* was huge and she deserved to enjoy every second of it. And she would.

She would also enjoy every second of Jeremy.

Bella dressed and dried her hair. She'd just finished packing her things up and wiping down the counter, when she heard his truck drive up. Her mother had left earlier that morning, and Bella was checking out of their rental house as well, opting to spend the last few days she had in town at Jeremy's apartment.

She closed the door behind her and walked down the sidewalk just as Jeremy hopped out of his truck.

He tucked his phone into his back pocket and greeted her with a warm smile and kiss on the cheek. "I'm sorry, Bella. I wanted to pick you up at the door, like a gentleman." He waved his arm dramatically down the sidewalk and she laughed.

"Not to worry. You are very much a gentleman."

"I needed to take that call," he explained. "It was the chief. He's been in touch with another fire chief on the East Coast. He's helping me line things up for Char. It shouldn't be too long now and we'll have her home."

"Oh, Jer. That's amazing. You must be so relieved."

"So much."

Bella could see the effort he made to keep things casual, but she'd noticed the strain his worry had caused him. He'd been under a huge amount of pressure trying to work things out for his sister, as anyone would be. "If you want to talk about—"

"You know what? I appreciate the offer. Really, I do. But I think today, the best thing to do is just enjoy my time with you. I've done everything I can today and having a great day with you will help me take my mind off things because there's nothing more I can do right now."

"I can definitely help distract you." She grinned and impulsively pressed up to her tiptoes to kiss him.

He dropped her bag and wrapped his arms around her in reflex, kissing her back. Hard.

"Ummm." Jeremy touched his fingers to his lips. "I like that kind of distraction. That was nice. It almost makes me want to cancel our plans and take you straight home." He wiggled his eyebrows and she laughed, smacking him playfully in the chest.

"No way." She shimmied her hips as she slipped by him on the sidewalk and made her way to the truck. "You told me you had a special day planned and I want *all* of it." She turned, her hand on the door handle. "Oh, and I want the special night, too."

Behind her, she heard him groan. "Oh, baby. I'll give you all the special you can handle."

Two hours later, special was only one of the words that Bella could use to describe what Jeremy had planned for them. She stood in a small clearing in the forest and looked straight up into the snow-covered pines that towered over her. The sun sparkled off the snow, creating a *special*, magical wonderland that they were right in the middle of. Jeremy had driven her out of town on the forestry back roads until they found a trailhead. He'd helped her into the snowshoes he'd brought for her and together they'd set off down the trail for a winter hike.

Bella had never been snowshoeing before, but it didn't take

her long to work it out. Once she got used to the large pieces of metal and plastic strapped to her feet, there was nothing to it. It was a gorgeous day. The sun was warm, flashing through the trees as they progressed down the trail.

"You're a natural," Jeremy said when Bella came to stand next to him where he waited for her.

"It's actually harder than it looks." Bella surprised herself by being out of breath. She always considered herself to be in pretty good shape, but snowshoeing took a completely different set of muscles than the ones she experienced doing the little bit of yoga she did.

"You're doing great." Jeremy touched her nose with his mittened hand and laughed. "And you are super cute when you're out of breath. In fact…" He leaned toward her to kiss her, but Bella ducked out of the way with a squeal.

"Oh no you don't." Awkwardly because of the giant snow-shoes strapped to her feet, Bella started to run down the path, giggling the entire way. "I'm not that easy to—"

Her words were lost as she tripped over her snowshoe and flew forward. She didn't even have time to worry about the landing as she propelled over her feet and landed face first into the snowbank next to the trail.

As soon as Bella started to run, Jeremy knew exactly how it was going to turn out. He'd had enough experience with snowshoes to know that it was never a good idea to try to run in them. Still, he couldn't help but smile and chase after her as she took off down the trail.

He didn't have to chase her very far, because just as he'd predicted, it didn't take long before she tripped over her clumsy feet and went flying through the air in a way that would have been actually pretty impressive, if he hadn't been concerned about how hard she landed.

"Bella!" Jeremy ran as quickly as he could manage in his shoes and dropped down to his knees in the snow next to her. "Bella, are you okay?" He took hold of her by the shoulders and lifted her up and over so she lay on her back in the snow. He was prepared for the worst; after all, she'd fallen pretty hard.

But to his surprise and shock, not only was she fine, she was laughing. Her entire body shook from the laughter she was trying—unsuccessfully—to contain, until finally it came spilling out in a burst.

"That was...oh my God...I can't believe that just happened." She laid back into the snowbank as her body convulsed.

Jeremy shook his head and laid back next to her, flipping his snowshoes out in front of him so they stood straight up. "I should have warned you," he said. "It's never a good idea to run in snowshoes because...well..." He waved his hand in the air. "That."

Next to him, Bella was overtaken by a fresh round of the giggles. "Well, you could have told me that," she said between breaths. "Not that it would have changed anything."

"Oh yeah?" Jeremy rolled over so he was propped up on an elbow and could look at her. "You still would have run from me?" He let one mittened hand run up her leg. Even bundled up in bulky winter gear, Bella was sinfully sexy and he couldn't keep his hands off her. At least, he sure didn't want to keep his hands off her. "I mean," he continued as his hand trailed farther up her body, "I'm all for the chase, because it makes the catching so much sweeter."

Her laughter dried up and her eyes darkened with desire as he positioned one arm over her, bracing him in the snow so he caged her in beneath him.

Bella's breath came fast, her chest rising and falling. But this time it wasn't humor causing it, but need and desire for him.

"I'll always let you catch me." Her words came out in a puff of air that he caught with his kiss as his lips crashed down on hers.

She groaned and her body squirmed beneath his. If only there wasn't a risk of frostbite, he'd have her stripped bare in an instant so he could worship her body properly. But there'd be time for that later. He'd make sure of it.

Reluctantly, Jeremy pulled away from her and rolled off into the snowbank next to her. He needed to cool off if they were ever going to make it out of the forest. And as much fun as they were having, there was still a lot more fun to be had. And it definitely wasn't going to involve thick snowsuits.

After a moment, he sat up again and looked at her face. Her skin pinked from a mixture of desire and the cold snow. She'd never looked more beautiful. "You're amazing, you know?" He stared at her intently, completely overwhelmed by his feelings for this girl.

She bit her bottom lip and looked him in the eyes. "You're pretty amazing yourself," she said seriously. "Thank you for this. I've never done anything like this before, and I love that you show me things and give me these experiences."

"Baby, I'd give you the world if I could."

"Well, I'll settle for the mountains and all you can show me in this corner of the world."

He couldn't help but be struck by her words. *This corner of the world?* Did she not think he could give her more than just this? *Could* he give her more? Hell yes, he could. He could give her love and a life and—

"This whole day. It's been amazing and really fun." She interrupted his thoughts. "Exactly what I needed. What *we* needed before things get crazy." Her smile dipped, the laughter of earlier only a memory now. "Jeremy, you know that I'm going to have to leave for a long time and we haven't really had a chance to talk about it yet, but it could be—"

"Shh." He put his mittened hand gently over her mouth. Maybe they did need to talk about things and what it was all going to look like, but more than anything, Jeremy didn't want anything to ruin their day. "We don't need to talk about that now."

"Jer, we're going to have to talk—"

"We will." He interrupted her. "We will talk about it soon, okay? Just not today. Let's just enjoy the day without any of that…" He didn't know how to finish the sentence.

Real life?

Serious stuff?

Reality?

Not that it mattered. Any way he put it, it would only darken their day. And that was the exact opposite of what Jeremy had planned for them.

"Besides," he said, forcing a lightness back into his voice. "The day isn't over. Not even close." He pushed himself up to his knees and offered a hand out to her. "We still have a few hours of daylight, and if we go down this trail for like five more minutes, there's a surprise."

"A surprise?"

Her face lit up and Jeremy grinned. If she was excited just hearing about a surprise, she would be completely ecstatic when she saw it.

"What is it?"

He laughed as she took his hand and he hauled her up to standing. "It wouldn't be a surprise if I told you about it. But I promise it's amazing. You won't be disappointed."

She narrowed her eyes and gave him a sly smile. "Okay." She wiped some snow from her arms. "I trust you."

"You do?"

Bella laughed again. "Of course I do." She gave up the futile exercise of trying to rid herself of the snow that clung to her and straightened up, a glimmer of mischief in her eyes. "Want to race?"

Jeremy's mouth dropped open and she laughed. "I'm kidding," she said. "But if we don't get going, I am going to freeze to death and won't be able to enjoy this surprise you're telling me about."

"Fair enough."

He led the way down the trail again, moving a little quicker than before. Because she had a point—she had taken a pretty big tumble into the bank, and she *was* covered in snow. If they didn't keep moving, Bella could get really cold. For a moment, he questioned the logic in continuing on at all. Maybe they should turn back and get to the car, where they could warm up? But...the surprise was really only a few minutes away and it would be worth it. He knew it. He looked back over his shoulder at her.

She smiled and waved. "I'm fine, Jer!"

He laughed at her mind reading ability and shook his head before focusing once again on the path in front of them.

A few minutes later, just as he'd predicted, they turned around a bend in the trail, and there it was. The surprise.

Jeremy turned quickly to catch Bella's reaction when she saw it for the first time and he wasn't disappointed.

Her mittened hands both flew to her mouth. She shook her head in wonder and after a moment looked at him. "Is that... how did it..."

Jeremy nodded.

"That's an actual waterfall?"

He nodded. "It's called Angel Falls."

"Angel?"

She didn't take her eyes off the waterfall that had frozen into a spectacular ice sculpture. It didn't matter how many

times Jeremy saw it, Angel Falls was one of the most spectacular winter sites around. His mom and dad had brought him
and Charlotte out there when they were kids, and ever since, it
was one of his favorite places. Glacier Falls right in town was
beautiful, but this was…special in a completely different way.

"See how it's frozen?" Jeremy pointed to the sides of the
ice. "It kind of goes out into—"

"Wings." Bella nodded the moment she saw it. "Like angel
wings?"

"Exactly." Jeremy walked a little closer to the ice. "In the
summer, it's just a waterfall. Pretty, of course, but not like this.
Somehow the water freezes just so over the rocks along the side
so it looks like wings. Cool, right?"

"Very cool." Bella joined him on the ice. They were
walking directly on the frozen stream. "Are we *on* the river?"

He laughed. "It's not a river really, but yes. It freezes solid
in the winter. In fact, if you were into ice climbing, you could
even climb up the waterfall."

Bella looked at him in wonder. "Have you done it?"

He shrugged. "A few times when I was younger. But I'm
not so much a rock climber. It turns out that I like to keep my
feet on the ground."

She laughed. "Me too, I think."

He wrapped an arm around her and pulled her close. "Are
you glad I brought you here?"

Bella didn't answer right away, but she snuggled in closer to
him, tucking her head into his shoulder. "So glad," she said
after a moment. "I'm going to remember this day for a long
time, Jeremy. Thank you."

He pulled her closer, enjoying the feel of her against his
body. "No need to thank me, Bella. And the day isn't over yet. I
still have one surprise in store for you. Only this one will be
warmer. I promise. In fact, if I know us, it will be downright
hot."

Chapter Eleven

THERE WAS VERY little question in Stephanie's mind that Travis Bishop was the man she needed.

For Lynx Creek.

That's what she needed Travis for. To be the general contractor who could be trusted to handle the work on her Lynx Creek project while she was on set. Nothing more. And maybe if she kept telling herself that, she'd actually believe it.

Maybe. She really did need to keep reminding herself about that particular point, because something about the man literally made her want to rip her clothes off and throw herself into his strong, muscly arms.

It was a disconcerting feeling but it was also one that was occupying way more of her thoughts than was probably normal or healthy.

From the moment she met him, Steph couldn't get the man out of her mind. It was getting a bit ridiculous, too, because it was starting to affect her sleep. Waking up in the middle of the night, twisted up in the sheets and the lingering feel of Travis's lips on hers—or at least what she imagined his lips would feel like, considering he'd never actually kissed her—was not conducive to a good night's rest.

Never in her life had she been hot and bothered about a man like this. Let alone one who she'd never even kissed. Or... really even knew at all. It was insane.

Which was exactly why she hadn't mentioned it to anyone yet. What would she say? That she was fantasizing over a man she barely knew and it was starting to reach the point of obsession, occupying all of her thoughts in all of her waking—and sleeping—moments? No. She couldn't tell anyone that. They'd look at her as if she were insane. And if it was Hope and Faith she confided in, they'd laugh at her. Because they knew Travis. He was a friend of theirs, or at least a friend of Logan and Levi's, which only made it worse. If she told her sisters about these crazy feelings, they'd likely tell the guys and then...what if it actually got back to Travis? She'd never be able to look him in the eyes again. She would be mortified for him to know that she was so attracted to him it was hard to breathe when they were in the same room. And what if he got embarrassed or refused to work with her because it was awkward?

No.

She needed him. And not in *that* way. Oh, but maybe she did.

Steph shook her head hard to keep herself from going down that line of thought, *again*.

She'd considered telling Bella about her new and completely annoying feelings for Travis. After all, she was pretty new to town as well, and she didn't know everyone the way almost every other single person seemed to. Besides, they were going to be working closely together, and Steph did trust her and consider her a friend. But again, she'd stopped herself on that level, too. Because Bella was still pretty green when it came to Hollywood and celebrity culture. What if she said something at the wrong time? Or what if she slipped and mentioned Travis in front of the wrong person and it got out? The press would have a field day with new gossip about her dating life.

She couldn't risk it getting out.

Any type of relationship news would take away from the movie itself, and that wasn't fair to the project or anyone else involved in it.

Besides, she was still getting over the breakdown of her last relationship. Well, not really, but it was definitely easier to use her very public break-up with Dax Combs as her excuse to the media—and for her friends, in some cases—for not moving on. The reality was, she hadn't really given the idea of a new relationship much thought.

Steph knew that there were a handful of her friends, and no doubt her sisters, who thought she'd be a great match with Nick Newton. And for a hot minute, she'd considered the idea, at least while he'd been hanging around Glacier Falls after Damon and Katie's wedding. Of all the men in town, Nick was...well, he was different. He was a bit nerdy, but sexy, too. And because of some kind of microchip he'd designed with Damon, ridiculously wealthy, which was always a good thing when it came to dating. Most men were intimidated by Steph's success and the wealth that went with it.

But Nick hadn't been. Not that it had gone anywhere. They'd flirted a bit and enjoyed hanging out together. Maybe it would have gone somewhere further except there'd been Faith and Logan's wedding, where a strange woman showed up with a baby that she'd claimed was Nick's.

Yeah. That was a lot for everyone to take in. Especially Nick, who'd taken off—with the baby—back to the city to sort things out.

Steph had tried to reach out a few times, and they chatted a little, but ultimately it had faded off.

Could it have been more?

Maybe. But even with Nick, she hadn't experienced the feelings anywhere like what she felt when Travis was around.

Steph exhaled slowly. Men were just a distraction and she had way too much that she wanted to accomplish to be distracted.

A new movie project.

A new building project at Lynx Creek.

Never mind the fact that she wanted to get to know her sisters better, and she was going to have a new little niece or nephew in a few short months.

All of those things were more important than a man. Even one as sinfully sexy as Travis Bishop.

"So, what do you think?"

"What?" Steph spun at the sound of the voice behind her. Travis's voice. He stood on the porch of the old lodge, directly behind where she'd been staring out over the frozen river, lost in thought. *About him.*

"Sorry," Travis added quickly. "I thought you heard me pull up. I didn't mean to scare you."

A flood of sensations flowed through her body, but fear wasn't one of them. She pulled herself together and pasted a bright smile on her face. "You didn't. I was just thinking about how amazing this will be in the summer." It wasn't a total lie. She did think about that every single time she visited Lynx Creek. She'd only seen pictures of the grounds in the summertime, having only discovered it a few months ago once the snow had already fallen. But if it was this spectacular in the winter, she knew it would be phenomenal in the summer.

"It is amazing." Travis had stepped up to stand beside her on the porch. He crossed his arms over his thick chest and gazed out over the snow-covered river along with her. "I'm not going to lie to you, Ms. Starz. I'm more than a little jealous that all this is yours."

Ms. Starz? She was going to protest the formal use of her name, but Travis was still talking.

"When I was a kid, my dad and grandfather would bring me here once a year for a three-generational fishing trip." He spoke to her, but he was clearly lost in the memories of those childhood experiences. "We only came about five or six times," he continued. "Up until the year my grandfather died. After that, my dad never picked up a fishing rod again."

There was sadness in his voice that drew her closer to him.

"Some of my best memories were on that river with both of them. The stories, the jokes," he said. "It was a special time." He nodded, almost to himself, and closed his eyes for a moment.

Steph tried not to stare at him, but she couldn't help it. She'd never before met a man who was so openly vulnerable with her so quickly after meeting her. She opened her mouth to say something. To acknowledge somehow what he'd just told her. But before she could, his eyes opened again and he turned to look at her. All traces of the seriousness of the moment were gone as he gave her a toothy grin. "You have something pretty incredible here."

Steph stuttered over words unsaid before finally forcing herself to nod. "Yes," she said simply. "I really do."

Steph spent the next two hours with Travis going from building to building, making extensive notes on each one and what work would need to be done specifically to bring them up to the quality Steph visualized.

"This one is actually in pretty decent shape," Travis said as they stood in the small two-room cabin. "Obviously it will need a little bit of work to bring it up to the standards you're creating, but it won't take long. And if you were going to consider staying on site, this might be a good choice."

"Staying on site?" Steph hadn't really considered the possibility of living at Lynx Creek while construction was going on. She was still at Ever After Ranch , but the house was going to get a little more crowded soon with the arrival of the new baby. Maybe it was a good option for when she came home after filming?

"You weren't going to?" Travis gestured around the small space with his free hand. The other held the clipboard he was using to take notes. "Sorry, I just assumed you were because of the supplies."

"Oh." She laughed. "Right. I totally forgot to mention it. My friend Jeremy asked me if he could use the cabin tonight." She shook her head because she still thought Jeremy was crazy when he'd asked her to use the little house for a romantic evening. For the life of her, Steph couldn't figure out what was romantic about a cold little cabin in the woods.

Sure, when she was finished with her renovations, the cabins would be plenty romantic, but now...

"That makes sense." Travis nodded. "I was wondering why there were stacks of blankets, pillows, and bottles of wine. It didn't really seem like the right type of supplies for you. And I didn't really think that you would—"

"That I would, what?" She tilted her head and stared at him. She put her hands on her hips. "You don't think I'd live here?"

She wouldn't. But not for the reasons he was thinking of, that were no doubt that she was too *fancy* or too *Hollywood*. And needed a higher standard of accommodation because she was so high maintenance. She wasn't. Nowhere near it. She wouldn't live there because if everything went to plan, she'd be gone for the majority of the construction, filming. But the mere fact that he assumed she was too good to live there felt like a challenge.

He shook his head. A sly grin that could only be described as a panty melter—because that's what it felt like was happening to her panties at that very moment—crossed his face. "No," he said simply. "I don't think you would."

"And why is that?"

"You need me to say it?"

She nodded.

"Because you are a fancy celebrity, Ms. Starz. Not a back country mountain girl. Not unless you're playing one in the movies." His words were sharp, but his blue eyes sparkled with mischief. He knew exactly what he was doing, playing with her. Challenging her.

And much to Stephanie's annoyance, it was working.

"You think I'm a fancy Hollywood type?"

"Definitely."

"So, five-star resorts, silk sheets, champagne breakfasts, that type of thing?"

"Sounds about right to me."

Sure, she'd enjoyed all of those things. Who wouldn't? Steph was far from pretentious, and she definitely remembered where she came from. But she also wasn't above enjoying the fruits of her hard work and everything they afforded her. And the truth was, being Hollywood's hottest celebrity definitely afforded her some of the finer things in life.

"Well then, I guess you'd be surprised to hear that I do in fact plan on staying here." The words were out of her mouth before she could think them through. She had absolutely *not* planned to stay on site.

Travis didn't even try to hide his surprise. "You are?" His mouth fell open. "Here? Out in the woods? By yourself?"

"When I'm in town. Yes." She nodded stubbornly, unable to stop herself. *What exactly was she trying to prove to this man?* "But not in this cabin," she said, surprised at her words. "I want the one closest to the river. It's tucked a little bit away from the lodge to still be private, but it's not too far away." As she heard the words come from her mouth, Steph realized that she did in fact want to live in the cabin. More than she expected. "It will get the morning sun on the porch, so I can sit and have a coffee while I watch the river. And then in the evening, the stars will be—"

"Like a blanket," he finished for her. "The other cabins will be nice, but they won't have the clear open view to the stars the way the bankside cabin will."

"Bankside?" A small smile tugged at her lips. "You named it?"

She couldn't have been more surprised to watch him duck his head with the slightest bit of embarrassment as he nodded.

"I kind of named it when I was a kid. We used to stay in that one."

"You did?" Steph was touched by his admission. "With your dad and grandfather?"

Travis nodded. "Sometimes we'd go out in the evening just as the sun was setting and the fish were feeding on the top of the water. We'd catch our dinner and then while Dad and Grandpa were cooking inside, and arguing about how much salt to use—it was always too much," he grinned at the memory, "I would sit out there and toss pebbles into the stream. I always tried to hit the bank on the other side."

"And did you?"

"Once." He nodded, lost in the memory. "It was the last time we came. I was about eleven. Two months later, just as the leaves were starting to turn, Grandpa had a heart attack. He died in his sleep and just like that, we quit fishing."

Steph took a step toward him, instinctively needing to comfort him. Despite the fact that they'd just met, she had the distinct feeling that Travis hadn't shared that memory before, and maybe he hadn't even allowed himself to think about it for quite some time. Either way, it felt like a special moment. She reached out to put her hand on his arm. "I'm really sorry—"

He turned and caught her hand in his so quickly, Steph hardly had time to process what was happening.

"No," was all he said. He held her arm up but didn't make a move to close the gap between them. His eyes held hers with so much intensity, he might as well have been pressed up against her body.

Her breath hitched and she gasped a little as he squeezed her hand ever so slightly before letting go.

"Don't be sorry," he said, the intensity gone, his light, teasing smile back on his face. "It's just life," he said simply. "Nothing to be sorry about."

Steph let her hand drop to her side. She nodded and called on all her training to fix a casual smile to her face. "Of course." Her voice was light and easy, a professional actress through and through. "It's just life."

She knew she put on a convincing performance, because she was damn good at what she did. It's too bad there weren't awards handed out for moments like this, because pretending that the little cabin they were standing in wasn't completely full of tension and passion and emotion of all kinds and that what had just happened between them wasn't something completely significant and altogether confusing at the same time, was, without a doubt, her best performance in a very long time.

Chapter Twelve

THE REST of the surprise Jeremy had in store *was* hot. But probably not the type of hot he'd had in mind when he'd teased Bella earlier. She couldn't help but laugh as the smoke billowed out of the little cabin only moments after Jeremy had lit a fire in the fireplace. Bella wasn't laughing because fire of any kind was funny. That wasn't it at all. But she couldn't resist the laughter when she saw his face after he realized there was something stuck in the chimney that was causing the smoke to vent into the small space instead of up and out the the roof. The irony of the situation was not lost on her, and once she started to laugh, she couldn't seem to stop herself.

It was definitely better for her to be outside and let Jeremy take care of the situation. She wasn't totally sure he'd appreciate her laughter.

Bella retreated to the porch of the tiny log cabin Jeremy had taken her to after their snowshoe adventure and let him deal with the fire and smoke problem inside. He was, after all, trained for such a situation. She tried not to smile at the sounds coming from inside, which included the occasional curse word. To distract her, Bella looked around.

The sun was starting to set behind the mountains, causing the snow-covered trees to glow a little. It all looked so magical. Bella was struck by the simple beauty of a place she had no idea existed. Her laughter fell from her lips as she took it all in. Her mouth opened into a small O, but no sound came out as the moment settled over her.

She was completely transfixed by the silence around them. It was a level of peacefulness she'd never experienced before. It settled into her bones in a way that almost made her cry. Bella closed her eyes and took a deep breath of the crisp, clean air mixed now with the comforting smell of woodsmoke.

"Hey." Jeremy's arms wrapped around her from behind and instantly warmed her when she didn't even realize she was cold. "I think I got it under control in there." He nuzzled into her neck. "Babe, you're freezing." He stepped back a bit and rubbed his hands up and down her arms.

Still, she couldn't pull her eyes away from the snow-covered trees. "It's so quiet out here."

"Right?" He held her close again, and Bella leaned back into his chest. "Do you like it? I hope it's not too quiet for—"

"No." A tear came to her eye, which was so ridiculous because she had absolutely no idea why. She'd just had the best day and had absolutely no reason to be sad.

Jeremy must have heard something in her voice, because he turned her in his arms and tilted her chin up with a finger. "What's wrong? I'm sorry I couldn't get the fire going. I just assumed...which is ridiculous. I should know better. You'd think that the new fire chief would—"

"Wait." She blinked hard. "Fire chief? What? Did you get the job and you didn't tell me?"

He was trying not to smile, but failing so miserably, Bella couldn't help but think it was the most adorable thing she'd ever seen. "Jeremy!" She smacked his chest playfully. "Start talking, buddy. Because if you're keeping secrets about—"

"It's not a secret." He caught her hand in his and held it. "Well, it is, I guess." His face clouded in momentary confusion. "I mean...it's freezing out here. Let's get inside where it's warm."

She let him lead her back into the cabin, which was now thankfully not nearly as smokey as it had been earlier. The fire crackled in the hearth, warming the small space and making it feel very cozy and welcoming.

Jeremy had brought in what seemed like piles of blankets and pillows, some of which he'd set up on the floor in front of the fire. He led her there now. "Warm up. You're freezing and I can't have you catching pneumonia or risking your voice."

Instinctively, Bella's hand reached for her throat and gave it a gentle rub. "I'm fine." She settled onto the blankets and crossed her legs before grabbing a pillow to hold in her lap. "But I won't be if you don't tell me what's going on. Did you get the fire chief job?"

Annoyingly, he didn't answer, but turned around and selected a bottle of red wine from the counter. He opened it and brought it, along with two glasses, to where she was sitting.

"Jeremy, I wouldn't say that I'm an impatient person, but..."

He laughed and poured her a glass that he handed her. "I'm not trying to torture you."

"Could have fooled me." She shook her head. Bella knew in her heart that Jeremy was going to get the fire chief job. How could he not? There was no one more devoted to the fire department than Jeremy, and she wasn't being biased, either. Everyone said so. The department had been Jeremy's whole life since he was a little kid. There was nothing he'd wanted more, and it wasn't just his *want* that made him perfect for the job. He genuinely cared about people. He would be one hundred percent fair, and always have the best interests of Glacier Falls in mind. Of that, there was no doubt. But that didn't mean she wasn't going a little bit crazy waiting for him to actually tell her the news.

"Okay," he finally said. "I'll tell you."

"You got it."

"It's not official."

That's all Bella needed to hear. She squealed and almost dumped her full glass of wine on him as she launched herself forward to give him a hug. "Of course you got it! I'm so proud of you."

"You know it's not official, Bella. I wasn't even supposed to say anything yet, but I couldn't not tell you, because…" He dropped his eyes, his face turning serious. "Because…well… Bella, because I can't imagine *not* telling you these things. I think I'm…no. That's wrong. I don't think anything. I *know.*" Jeremy cleared his throat and took the glass of wine from her hand before she could take a sip.

Her stomach clenched in a tight ball and her breath came fast. They'd only been dating about a month, and half of that time, she hadn't even been in town. But still, she knew what he was going to say. She sucked in a breath, ready to say the words in return.

He cupped her cheeks with both hands and looked her straight in the eye. "Bella, I know it's fast, but I know how I feel, and I just think life is too short not to just…"

"I totally agree."

"You do?"

She nodded, barely able to contain her own excitement. "I do."

"Oh, thank God." He took a deep breath and released it with a shake of his head.

She could hardly wait for him to say it. The words were on the tip of her tongue, too.

"Because, Bella, I'm totally in love with you."

The words fell off his tongue and rushed through her. She

closed her eyes and let herself revel in the moment. Bella was so completely consumed by what she was feeling for this man in front of her that it took her a second to come back to reality and realize he was still speaking and she'd totally missed what he was saying. But it didn't matter.

"Yes!" she blustered out. "I love you, too. And—"

"Yes?"

"Of course." Bella laughed. "It's just always felt so right with you."

Jeremy sat back on his heels. His eyes darkened with the seriousness of the moment. "So, you'll marry me?"

He had no idea he was going to ask her to marry him. He hadn't planned it. Not even a little. Hell, he hadn't even thought about it himself. Not really. Not in any kind of serious way. But being there with her...declaring his love for her...it just felt right. And after hearing about the chief job and with Bella's movie role...it was perfect. It was all perfect. Everything was lining up and it just felt right, so he said it.

And then she'd said yes.

Hadn't she?

There was a flicker of surprise in her eyes when he asked her again. No, it was more than a flicker. It was downright shock.

"Bella?"

He grabbed her hands. "I just thought...."

"Sorry." She pulled her hands away and ran them through her hair. "I don't mean to...I was just..." She looked down at her lap and when she looked up again, she was laughing. "It was a long day, and I think maybe the wine went straight to my head."

He looked at her completely untouched glass. She hadn't even had a sip yet, but he didn't see the point in mentioning it.

"I could have sworn you just asked me to marry you and that would be the most insane thing because—"

"Would it?"

The look on her face told him everything he needed to know. It *would* be insane. At least she thought it would be.

She stood and walked to the window. "Jeremy," she said after a moment before turning around. "Of course it would be."

No. It wouldn't be. He felt that in his bones. It wasn't insane to want to be with the one person you were completely connected with. Sure, societal norms might think it was crazy, but that didn't matter.

He jumped to his feet and moved to stand in front of her.

"It's not crazy," he said slowly. "When you know, you know."

"I'm about to go off and shoot a movie, Jeremy." Her voice rose an octave. "You're about to get busy with your new promotion, too. This just isn't a good time."

He laughed. He couldn't help it. "Is it ever a good time? I bet you could ask Faith and Hope what they have to say about that. There's never a good time to get married. Not really. Look at all the weddings they've done last minute, or randomly. I bet they'd agree. The only thing that matters is love."

She opened her mouth but closed it again before speaking.

He was torn. Maybe he shouldn't push her on the issue. Obviously he'd taken her off guard. And maybe he shouldn't have sprung it on her the way he did. He probably could have eased her into the idea, but…no.

Fuck it.

He said exactly what he was feeling and that was always the best policy. Wasn't it?

"Bella, I know it's a lot. And…" He blew out a breath.

"Don't answer me right now, okay?" The look in her eyes could only be described as relief and instantly, Jeremy knew he made the right choice. After all, she hadn't said no outright, and that was a good sign. He took her hand in his and this time, she didn't pull away. "Let's just enjoy the rest of our night, okay?"

She didn't hesitate in her response. "Yes." The beautiful smile returned to her face, followed by the sparkle in her eyes. "Besides, we need to celebrate someone's promotion. Official or not," she added before he could protest again. "Besides, you know it will be soon."

He couldn't argue with that.

Together, they moved back to sit in front of the fireplace, where they toasted and drank to Jeremy's soon-to-be promotion. They were halfway through the bottle before Jeremy pulled out the picnic-style dinner he'd prepared. Or more accurately, had Brody put together. While they ate, Bella filled him in on the updates to the script she'd just received, and she promised to let him hear her practicing the songs for the soundtrack as soon as she felt confident with the lyrics, which would have to be soon, because the studio had decided that the best way to start the promotion machine going early for the movie was to introduce Bella Burton to the world with a showcase of a selection of songs from the film.

"They're going to do that before even starting to shoot?" Jeremy didn't pretend to know anything at all about the movie business, but the more he heard about Bella's project, the more he realized it was going to be a pretty big deal.

"I know, right?" Bella practically bounced talking about it. "And it's going to be in like two weeks."

"What? When did you hear about all of this?" He tried not to be hurt that she hadn't mentioned any of this before, but then again, they'd both been pretty preoccupied in the last few days.

"Lewis mentioned it as a possibility awhile ago, but they

just confirmed today." She grinned. "I know I said I wouldn't look at my phone, but I snuck a little look on the drive over here." She was so excited that Jeremy couldn't be upset with her, even though he had suggested a *tech-free* night, just the two of them. But then again, it likely wasn't very practical with everything going on.

He shrugged and admitted, "I looked at mine too. I was hoping for an update on Char."

"That totally makes sense. We have a lot going on."

He kissed her again. "That we do, babe. I'm just glad we have this time together right now."

"Mmm."

She moaned against his lips and instantly, Jeremy's cock was hard. She turned him on so easily. His body responded perfectly to her.

"It's going to get crazy, Jeremy." Bella broke the kiss and his hopes that he would be getting her naked in the next few minutes. "I'll be in LA for months, and—"

"I can't wait to visit," he said casually. He traced a hand up her leg to rest in the dip of her waist. He worked his fingers beneath the fabric of her sweater and splayed his hands on her bare skin as he spoke. "I've always wanted to go to LA. The Hollywood sign? Universal Studios? You bet, I'm in."

"Really?" She looked up at him. "You'll come visit?"

"I'll be there so much you'll get sick of me." He bent and pressed his lips to hers again. This time, moving his hand farther up her body as his kiss grew more urgent.

"Never." She grinned wickedly and bit her bottom lip. "And I'll never get sick of the way you kiss me."

"And that's all I needed to hear."

She squealed as he moved over her, pressing her flat on her back and kissing her in such a way that left no more room for conversation.

Chapter Thirteen

"TELL me again how they were able to pull this off in only a few days." Bella looked around the barn at Ever After Ranch for at least the sixth time, taking in all the new details as she let her eyes travel the room. It had been less than twenty-four hours since Bella and Jeremy had emerged from the woods and their romantic night in the cabin. After they'd confessed to each other that they'd both looked at their phones, they made a big show of turning them off and putting them away until they drove back down into town and Sweetie Pies for a morning coffee.

When they'd turned on their phones, they'd both been surprised to hear that later that evening there was to be a baby shower for Hope and Levi and, according to the email invitation, *they better be there.*

Not that Bella would want to miss it. Not for anything. She was only just starting to develop friendships with both Hope and Levi. They were great people and even if she didn't know them, Jeremy was close with them. And their baby…well, it was like a miracle. And most definitely deserved a celebration. And what a celebration it was. Ever

After Ranch was known for weddings, but after this production, maybe they'd have to start venturing out into baby showers.

Because Hope and Levi didn't know the sex of the baby yet, the decorations were all done in neutrals of creams and browns with a teddy bear theme. Everything had a rustic, yet soft feel. There were clusters of candles on all surfaces, and teddy bears of all sizes piled as centerpieces. Everything was very cute, but very classy at the same time. Very much like Hope herself.

"It's pretty amazing, isn't it?" Bella sat with Katie and Sarah. They'd claimed a table and were enjoying a quick catch-up in the middle of the festivities, and more accurately, enjoying a selection of the food Brody and the staff at Birchwood had prepared.

Katie lifted a smoked salmon roll and licked her lips. "And the food…your husband is amazing." She popped the appetizer into her mouth and closed her eyes with a groan as she chewed.

"Hey," Sarah said. "I'm the only one he's allowed to make groan like that."

Katie laughed so hard she almost spat out her food.

Bella didn't even try to hide her smile. "Still," she said. "This food…*all* his food is amazing."

"Right?" Sarah turned to face her. "Brody said he made you and Jeremy a special picnic dinner for last night. What was that all about?"

"Ohh, sounds romantic." Katie grabbed another treat from the plate in front of her. "A picnic? In the winter?" She put a mini quiche in her mouth. "Not going to lie, it sounds cold."

"Well…" Bella debated how much to tell her new friends. "We actually stayed in one of the little cabins at the old fishing camp."

"Lynx Creek cabins?" Katie said through a mouth full of

food before covering it with her hand. "Sorry, I'm starving. I have no idea why."

"Pregnant." Sarah said it so casually, Bella's mouth fell open.

But Katie shook her head and rolled her eyes. "Nope. No babies here." She patted her flat stomach. "At least not for a bit. I'm way too busy with the store right now. There is no time for a baby."

"Like a baby cares how busy you are." Sarah shook her head. "I mean, you do know that's not how it works, right?"

Bella watched with wonder as the two of them discussed what could be a potential life changer for Katie, who seemed way too calm if there were a possibility that she could be pregnant.

"Nope," Katie said again. "Not preggo. Now, I want to hear about this romantic picnic in a cabin." And just like that, the attention was back on Bella. "Spill."

Bella shrugged. "It was nice." That was lame and she knew she should give her friends a little bit more, but at the same time she didn't want to tell them too much. Or more specifically, she didn't want to tell them that Jeremy had...what had he done? He hadn't proposed. Not really. At least, she *hoped* that wasn't a proposal. Sure, maybe she wasn't a diehard romantic, but still, she wanted a bit more effort than that. Even so, he had definitely brought up marriage. And even though there hadn't been much time to think about it yet, or what it meant, Bella wasn't so sure how she felt about the whole thing.

Marriage?

They hadn't even been dating a full month. Getting married was crazy. *Right?*

She needed to think about it. On her own. But what she did *not* need to do was talk about it with the ladies. No doubt they'd have some pretty strong opinions about it all. Even though there was still a lot Bella didn't know about them, she did know that all the women of Glacier Falls had opinions on *all* the things. Especially when it came to relationships and marriage.

They were sitting in *the* wedding venue, for goodness' sake.

No. She definitely wasn't going to tell anyone about the whole *marriage* thing.

"It was really nice," she offered instead. "We had a fun day snowshoeing and then the cabin. It was all…really romantic. And absolutely perfect since I have to head back to the city tomorrow. It's all happening so fast."

"Oh my goodness." Sarah bounced in her chair. "Tell us about the movie. I knew you were leaving soon, but tomorrow? That's so fast."

"That's why we had to have this shower so fast." Faith joined the ladies at the table. She held a tray of cupcakes, all of which had a little teddy bear made out of modeling chocolate perched on top of a cloud of what looked like very delicious icing.

"Is that why you had it so last minute?" For half a second, Bella was touched by the gesture, until she remembered that Steph was Hope's half-sister, and she, too, would be leaving for the city the following day. So if they held the shower early, it was because of that, *not* her. She almost laughed out loud at herself.

"Of course." Faith put the tray down and sat across from Bella. "We wanted all of you here."

It was a really nice thing to say, and it wasn't lost on Bella, who offered her new friend a smile of gratitude.

"And I have a feeling that this baby is going to come early," Faith added. "I mean, if she's anything like my twin sister, she's going to be a pain in the ass."

"I am *not* a pain in the ass." Hope, in her decorated wheel-chair—a surprise from Steph, who now pushed her around—

arrived at the table just in time to hear her twin sister's comment.

Faith winked at Bella before turning to her sister. "Hope? I didn't see you there."

"Yeah, right." Hope laughed. "And you're right, I am a pain in the ass." She smiled sweetly at her identical sister. "But I'm *your* pain in the ass."

"For better or for worse, right?" Faith groaned. "Oh wait, that's something else."

Bella couldn't help but feel a twinge of...something...at her choice of words.

"Well, I'm glad I could be here for you, Hope," Bella said quickly. "Congratulations. I can't wait to meet the little guy."

"Or girl," Steph added quickly. "I'm convinced the baby is going to be a girl. With red hair, like her favorite auntie." Steph twirled her hair around her finger and laughed. They may be genetically connected, but Steph's signature red hair came from her father's side. The girls all shared a very blonde—just like the twins—mother.

"Oh, you're totally right, Steph." Faith took a cupcake off the tray she'd brought. "But the little jellybean *is* going to look just like her favorite auntie."

Everyone laughed as they each selected cupcakes for themselves and raised them in a toast.

"Seriously," Faith said when they all had a treat. "I'm so excited for you, Hope. The little jellybean is already so loved. I can't wait until he—*or* she—gets here."

"To Hope."

"Cheers."

"To Jelly Bean!"

They all *toasted* their cupcakes and took big bites full of frosting right as the men walked up to join the group.

Jeremy gave Bella a wink as she struggled with her mouthful of cake. A mouthful of cake she very nearly choked on when Logan said, "I understand there might be another wedding at Ever After soon."

Logan wasn't supposed to say anything.

Hell.

Jeremy shouldn't have even told him that he'd sort of, not really proposed to Bella. Because it wasn't a proposal—it was more of a *putting it out there*. Not that he would have been upset if she'd immediately agreed to the idea. Not at all.

Either way, Jeremy didn't know why he'd told the guys about the whole *let's get married* thing, except of course for the fact that he was super excited about the idea and now that he'd actually said it out loud, he couldn't think of anything else but making Bella his wife. He had to tell someone, and when they got to the party and everyone was there, most of his friends paired up with wives of their own, well...he couldn't really help it.

So, maybe he did know why he'd said something.

Still. Logan was *not* supposed to say anything. None of them were supposed to say anything.

"What?"

"Married?"

"No way!"

"Bella?"

"So exciting!"

All the women spoke at once. All except one.

Everybody had turned to stare, open-mouthed, at Bella. Everyone except Stephanie, who watched Jeremy silently. Her lips pressed into a thin and somewhat unimpressed line.

And of course Bella, herself, looked at him with an expression he couldn't fully read.

It only took her a second to compose herself. "I don't know if now is the right time to—"

"Now is a great time." Katie spoke up. She beamed at Jeremy.

They had a history, and he knew that it was ancient history and she only wanted the best for him. No doubt, she was thrilled with this news.

"You guys are getting *married?*" She looked between them both.

Jeremy simply shrugged but he couldn't have wiped the smile off his face if he'd tried. Sure, they hadn't made any official plans and really, they hadn't even finished the conversation the night before, but *yes* of course they were going to get married. Maybe not right away, but...

"Really," Bella said. "I don't think we should talk about this now. It's Hope and Levi's big day. I hate it when big news is announced at someone else's event. It's not really fair." She turned to look at Hope and gave her a small smile. "I'm so sorry. This is your day. Well, it's Jelly Bean's day," she added. "Nothing should take away from that."

Hope and Bella exchanged a few words, but Jeremy wasn't listening because all he could focus on was two words that Bella had said.

Big news.

"You know what," Jeremy blurted out. "Bella is absolutely right. Like always." He winked at her, but her face was still unreadable. "We don't want to take any attention away from what's really important right now." Jeremy turned to Hope and Levi, who'd moved to stand behind his wife. "Today is all about the both of you and your little bundle. Our *news* can wait."

There were a few more mumbled questions and comments, but for the most part, everyone moved on in different conversations. He moved to go to Bella, but Katie grabbed him and pulled him aside before he could reach her.

"Marriage? What?" She smacked him in the arm and pulled him into a hug. "I did not see that coming," Katie said when she released him. "I mean, I know you are totally head over heels for Bella. Anyone can see that. But I did not think you guys would jump straight to marriage."

"Well, it's not like we've decided on—"

"Will you wait until after the movie has filmed, or do it right away? I mean, doesn't she start right away? Oh, wow. You're going to be so busy," Katie continued to gush.

Jeremy tried not to be rude, as he attempted to catch Bella's eye. But Steph had pulled her into a conversation and they were looking at their phones and not in his direction at all.

"Congratulations, man."

Jeremy turned his attention back to the conversation at hand as Damon joined them.

He wrapped an arm around his wife and pulled her close. "And good move, too. When you know what you want, make sure you go for it so she doesn't get away." He kissed Katie's forehead. "I got lucky, but not everyone does," Damon continued. "And I've been to those Hollywood parties…" He shook his head and let out a low whistle. "It's probably not a bad idea to lock it down before she gets super famous and—"

"Lock it down?"

"Damon. That's a terrible thing to say."

Damon held up his hand in defense. "I don't mean anything by it. It's just that…well, it would take a pretty confident man to let his woman into that world without even a little bit of concern. That's all I'm saying. And I'm for sure not the only one thinking it."

Katie and Damon drifted off into a different conversation, but it didn't matter; Jeremy wasn't paying any attention to them. He only had eyes for Bella.

Bella was only half listening to what Steph was talking about. She glanced down at the calendar on her friend's phone. Steph was pointing at some colored squares and spaces, but for the life of her, Bella had no idea what she was saying or what she was talking about. She looked up at her friend's face and focused.

"Rehearsal...recording...showcase..."

Okay. Bella's brain caught up. Steph was going over the schedule for the next few weeks. *Yes.* She worked hard to focus on what she was saying. Steph had pulled her away from the crowd moments after Jeremy's...*what?* His revelation? His announcement?

His...whatever it was.

And Bella was grateful for Steph knowing exactly what she needed. Which at that particular moment was space. And distraction. Even though the distraction technique wasn't working at all.

Bella's eyes kept moving up to watch Jeremy, who was deep in conversation with Damon and Katie. They were laughing and smiling, and Bella had no doubt they were talking about the whole marriage thing.

Marriage thing.

What the hell? Where had that all come from?

The night before, Bella had kind of thought he was joking. Well, maybe not joking, but at least that it would be a conversation between them at some point. Not something that needed to be blurted out to the whole group. Hell, she hadn't said anything to the ladies. Because... well, because there was nothing to tell. Certainly not that they were actually getting married!

"Hello? Are you even listening to me?"

Bella blinked hard and tore her gaze away from Jeremy.

She refocused on Steph, who looked at her with a mixture of concern and humor.

"Sorry. I was just…"

"Oh yeah. I get it." Steph tucked her phone away. "Which is exactly why I'm trying, and failing, to distract you with this. Do not let yourself get distracted with any of that right now," Steph commanded.

Bella's shoulders fell. "How can I not? Did you hear him? Did you—"

"Oh, I did." Steph crossed her arms. "And I totally get why you can't focus right now." She looked in Jeremy's direction, shook her head sharply, and looked back to Bella. "What I don't know is what exactly Jeremy was thinking."

Bella wanted to scream with relief. Finally, someone who recognized this whole thing and the timing of it all was completely insane.

But before she could say anything, Steph continued, "Married? Now? Do you think his timing could be worse? I mean, he's not really serious, is he?" She shook her head. "No, don't answer that. The two of you need to talk. But I don't think now is a good time. You really should be focusing on what's about to happen. You shouldn't have any distractions at all."

Her friend was right. Bella did need to be concentrating on her career, and everything that was about to go down. Tomorrow. First thing in the morning, they would be leaving to go back to the city, where Lewis had rehearsals and voice lessons and recording sessions all lined up for Bella to begin immediately. She really didn't have time to think about anything else. Not if she wanted to focus and do the very best job she could with the movie. Which she did.

Shit was about to get real. Very real.

She did not have the mental capacity to be thinking about a marriage proposal, if that's even what it was. "You're exactly right." Bella nodded, freshly focused. "Let me see that schedule. I need to—"

"Bella, can we talk for a minute?"

She turned at the sound of Jeremy's voice. The man had nothing if not perfect timing. He looked to Steph apologetically, but then his gaze homed right back in on Bella.

"I'm sorry, I know you're busy talking about..." He shrugged because he obviously had no idea at all what they were talking about. "Please, can we talk for a quick minute?"

Bella looked to Steph.

"No distractions," her friend repeated. "This is important." Steph turned and walked away, leaving them alone before either of them could respond.

As soon as they were alone, Jeremy took her hand and gave it a squeeze. And just as it always did, her body responded instantly to him. She felt herself leaning in closer to him.

Her heart fluttered at his touch. No matter what crazy stuff he was talking about right now, the man did know how to get a reaction out of her. And it really didn't take much.

He led her to an empty table. The moment they sat down, Bella looked at him and said, "What the hell, Jeremy? You told everybody we were getting married? We haven't even really—"

"I know." He interrupted her. "And I know that it doesn't sound like it, but I promise I did *not* tell them we were getting married. I didn't," he added when she cocked an eyebrow. "I was just, I don't know. The guys were all talking, and I was so excited about the night we had last night. And how special it was and how close to you I felt. And...I just blurted it out. And maybe it sounded like...okay, it probably did sound like we were actually—"

"Getting married?" Bella finished for him. She pulled her hand away from his. She could not be touching him and having this conversation. She could not be touching him and be angry at him at the same time, if that's what this was, and it was. It hit her like a flash. She *was* angry.

She hadn't even realized it up until that exact moment.

But she *was* angry. That he'd said something at all. Not only was it the absolute worst time, at a baby shower, but more importantly, it wasn't true. They weren't getting married.

No distractions.

"I can't believe you did that, Jeremy." She shook her head. "Do you understand what kind of position that puts me in? What am I supposed to say? That we're not getting married? 'Cause we're not." She made a point to add that important detail. But at the look of his crestfallen face, she couldn't help herself but to add quickly, "At least not yet. This is all still so new, Jeremy."

He nodded. "I know. But is it really so crazy? I mean, crazier things have happened, right, Bella?"

What was he saying? Of course it was crazy.

"I mean, why not? I love you. You love me."

She nodded. Because yes…he did. She did. But that didn't mean that they were supposed to get married.

Jeremy was still talking. "And you're about to go off, and have this great adventure. Which is great," he added quickly. "But I just don't want you to…"

She sat back in her chair, not sure she wanted to hear him finish the sentence but knowing she needed to. "What? You don't want me to what?"

Jeremy took a breath and exhaled slowly. "It's not like you're going to…" He shook his head. "This is all coming out wrong."

"Just say it."

He dropped his chin to his chest for a moment. "I guess I was just thinking that maybe, you'd go off to Hollywood and get to a party and meet someone rich and famous and I'd be back here and…I mean, do you really have to go?"

Bella felt as though she'd been slapped. She blinked. Hard. "What?" She shook her head in an effort to clear it. Maybe she hadn't heard him properly. Because surely he hadn't really asked her not to follow her dreams. No. He wouldn't. "Did you just…"

"No," he said quickly. "I'm not saying anything. I was just…I mean, there's a lot for you right here in Glacier Falls, too. You know that, right?"

Of course she knew that. But…this was her career. It was the biggest break she could ever hope to get and…

"Marry me, Bella."

Not this again. Not like this.

"Marry me and stay here in Glacier Falls."

She shook her head. There was no way he'd just said that. *No way.*

"You don't have to go to Hollywood to have a great life. You don't need to do this."

"This?"

"The movie. The acting. The whole thing. You can have a full life right here with me."

This wasn't Jeremy. This wasn't the man she had fallen in love with. No way. He would never…

"Look around you, Bella." Jeremy's voice had taken on an almost manic quality. He spoke so fast, she could barely keep up with what he was saying. "Everyone here is happy. They have each other, they're in love, they—"

"Aren't me."

He shook his head. "No. They aren't. But—"

"You aren't really asking me to choose, Jeremy, are you?"

"Choose?"

No distractions.

"Between you and my career." She hoped he wasn't doing that. More than anything, she hoped he wasn't going to make her choose. Her heart squeezed in her chest. "Please don't make me—"

The sharp ring of his cell phone interrupted them. Bella wanted him to let it go to voicemail, but she knew that he couldn't do that.

And he didn't.

She watched while Jeremy pulled his phone out of his pocket. "It's…shit." He looked up at her. "I'm sorry, it's the chief."

She nodded and he took the call. She waited and tried to gather her thoughts while Jeremy talked—or more specifically —listened to the call.

"I'm sorry," he said a moment later. "It's Char." He was already up and out of his seat. "She's on her way. I have to go."

Chapter Fourteen

IT WAS all happening so soon. Jeremy wasn't ready. Not that it mattered. As soon as Ed Walker called to say that Charlotte was safely on a plane and headed to him, and home, there was nothing that was going to keep him from hopping in his car and driving the two hours to the city to meet her at the airport and bring her home. For good.

Nothing.

The image of Bella flashed through his mind.

Even Bella.

No. That wasn't true. Bella would never have made him choose between her or his sister. Not the way he was asking her to choose.

Was he asking her to choose?

He didn't even know what had come over him earlier. What was he saying? He'd gotten caught up in the moment of being there with everyone who had what he wanted to have and...*dammit.* Had he really told her that she didn't need to go do the movie?

He had.

But had he meant it?

That was a harder question to answer. At least to answer honestly.

She'd asked him outright whether he was going to make her choose. But he didn't have the chance to answer her.

"Go," Bella had said. "Go make sure she's safe." Because Bella never would have told him to stay.

And so he had. Because there was really no other choice. But he couldn't get the image of Bella in the Ever After barn, that look on her face as if he'd just screwed up in an epic way and there was no coming back from it, out of his head. She looked at him like…it might be the last time.

No.

He couldn't even let himself think that way. They'd had an argument. It wasn't even an argument. It was more like a disagreement. A difference of opinion. And if they'd had time to talk it through, it would have been cleared up. It's just that he'd had to leave and…yes. It would be fine. What he had with Bella was stronger than whatever had just happened at the baby shower. So much stronger.

But still, doubts filled his head as Jeremy drove. So many doubts.

At least thinking about Bella took his mind off the situation with his sister. But the moment he parked at the airport, and ran to the gate, just as the flight was letting out, the only thoughts he had space for were for Charlotte.

As soon as she appeared from the sliding doors, her blonde hair pulled back into a messy ponytail, nothing more than a backpack and a small purse across her unusually thin body, Jeremy ran forward, all but pushing the other passengers out of the way, and pulled her into an embrace.

She resisted at first. Her body instinctively stiffened. But only a few seconds later, she melted into his hug and he felt her relax.

They stood that way for a long time. Jeremy had no idea

how long had passed, but finally a security guard, obviously sensitive enough to see they were having a moment, tapped him on the shoulder and gently asked them to move on.

It wasn't until they were in the car driving back to Glacier Falls and Charlotte was staring out the window at the snow that had started to fall while they'd been inside, that Jeremy asked, "Are you okay?"

It should have been a simple question, but they both knew it was anything but.

Slowly, she turned from the window and gave him a small smile full of pain. "I will be."

"Yes." He nodded. "You will be. I'll make sure of it."

They didn't speak again for a few minutes, each lost in their own thoughts about everything that had happened. Ed had filled Jeremy in that although they weren't planning to move forward with the plan for a few more weeks still, things escalated when Billy seemed to catch on that something was going on with Char.

Apparently, Charlotte hadn't behaved any differently, but Billy's paranoia brought on these periods of mania periodically. And this time, because they were actually planning something, both Char and the fire chief in Halifax were concerned that he'd actually discover something and do something to harm Charlotte before they had a chance to get her out safely.

They couldn't risk it. So they'd moved forward with the plan and when Charlotte had shown up for work at the coffee shop that afternoon, Joe Black was waiting for her. He ordered a coffee and a blueberry muffin, which was their prearranged code that it was time to go. Charlotte had grabbed her coat from the back and together they'd walked out the front door and to his waiting car.

They had contacted the local police force to keep an eye on Billy and make sure he didn't leave work early. He hadn't and everything had gone smoothly. Almost too smoothly. Not that anyone actually thought that was the end of it.

No.

There was no way Billy was going to give up so easily. But at least Char would be back home and where they could all keep her safe.

After they'd been driving for about thirty minutes in quiet, Char finally spoke. "Tell me about your girlfriend."

Jeremy glanced over at her, but kept his gaze steady on the snowy highway. "Really? You don't want to—"

"The last thing I want to talk about is how much I've screwed up my own life."

She laughed, but it was a humorless sound that tugged at Jeremy's heart. *How long until he got his sister back both in body and in spirit?*

"Tell me about her. I need to hear something good."

He pressed his lips together. There was a lot he could say, specifically that he wasn't really sure how he'd left things with her earlier that night and that maybe he'd screwed everything up right when it was starting to get good. But he was pretty sure his sister didn't need to hear any of that. Instead, he filled the time telling her about how talented Bella was, the movie role she'd just landed, and all the highlights of their relationship up until the argument they'd left it at a few hours earlier.

At some point, Charlotte had fallen asleep while Jeremy spoke. No doubt she'd been so tense she'd been unable to properly rest for who knows how long. His heart ached for his sister, who'd gone through things he couldn't even fathom and may not ever properly understand or ever really know about. She'd talk if and when she was ready, and until then, he'd be there for her. Reliving the past was no longer the important part.

The only thing that mattered was that she was home and safe.

It was almost midnight when Jeremy finally pulled up in

front of their childhood home. He put the car in park and sat in the silence for a few minutes until Charlotte instinctively woke up.

She blinked and rubbed at her eyes before looking out the window. "Oh."

"We're here."

She turned slowly toward him. "Thank you."

"Are you serious?" Jeremy unbuckled his belt and moved to open the door, but Char's hand on his arm stopped him.

"Wait."

He turned back.

"Will you stay?"

"Stay?" He nodded. "Of course. I'll tell Mom and Dad what—"

"No." She stopped him. "I know this is silly and I have no right to ask you this, but…" She dropped her head.

"Char? What is it? What do you need? You know I'll help you."

"It just all feels…" She looked up, her eyes still empty and dry from the tears he knew would come later. "I'd feel better if you stayed at the house tonight."

There was no hesitation. Jeremy nodded. "You know I'll do anything for you."

"Thank you. Really. I will never be able to—"

"You don't have to. None of that matters. I'm just glad you're here now. We'll keep you safe, Char. It's going to be okay."

She stared into his eyes so deeply, he felt as though she were searching for an answer he might hold the secret to. Finally, she nodded once, but didn't agree with him.

Together, they walked to the front door. Despite the late hour, there were still lights on in the kitchen and the study. From what his dad had told Jeremy, they were staying up later and later—both of them worried and unable to get the rest they needed, but unable to do anything to fix the situation.

Jeremy hoped they would all be able to rest easier now that Charlotte was home.

He knocked twice before opening the door and calling out, "Mom? Dad?"

They stepped inside and just as Jeremy had expected, his mother came out of the kitchen, a towel in her hand at the same time that their father appeared from the den, where he'd no doubt been working on tying some new flies for summer fishing.

"Jeremy? What on—Charlotte." His mother, Darlene, froze mid-sentence. The towel she held fell from her hand as she ran toward her daughter and without a moment's hesitation pulled her into a tight hug. "Oh, thank goodness you're home."

Darlene smoothed Char's messy ponytail over and over with her hand and she held her tight. His almost-six-foot-tall sister became a little girl in front of his eyes as she melted into her mother's embrace.

His father came up beside her and put a hand on his shoulder. There were tears in Dwayne's eyes when Jeremy turned to look at his dad. "Thank you, son."

There were no words that were even remotely adequate. Jeremy nodded, took a deep breath, and went to the kitchen to make a pot of coffee. It was going to be a long night of catching up.

Bella waited up at Jeremy's apartment for him to return from rescuing his sister. Not that she'd expected him to return that night. Not really. After all, she had no idea what was actually involved in getting Charlotte home safely. She had no expectations.

But she would have been lying if she said despite that, she was still disappointed to wake up the next morning alone in his bed.

The timing was terrible. There was still so much left unsaid between them. But she had to go. Steph was picking her up at six so they could get on the road early and Bella could get to the studio for rehearsal before ten.

She'd picked up her phone and set it down without typing a message to Jeremy half a dozen times the night before. She hadn't wanted to bother him or distract him from what he was doing with his sister. But truthfully, she didn't even know what to say to him.

He'd all but ambushed her with the marriage thing. And even if they did have a chance to properly discuss it, Bella was feeling less and less as if they were on the same page, and that scared the hell out of her.

"Do you really have to go?"

His words had played on repeat in her head all night.

Was that who Jeremy was? Had she just not seen it? Was he the kind of guy who would really ask her to give up her dream, to stay with him in Glacier Falls?

It seemed he was.

So, without ever sending a text to him, Bella packed up the last of her bags and right before she left, she placed her key on the counter with a quick note.

Hope it went well.
  ~Bella

She knew she should say more, but for the life of her, she couldn't think of one other thing to say. So she'd locked the door behind her, and walked to the waiting car Steph had arranged to drive them back to the city.

"You want to talk about it?" Steph asked halfway into their drive.

Bella turned away from the window and looked at her friend. "No." She turned back to resume her watching of the passing trees and mountains. There was nothing to talk about.

No distractions.

In only a few hours, she was going to be in the studio for the first time to lay down the first tracks of what could be the biggest moment in her career. That was the only thing she needed to focus on.

She'd turned her phone off and dropped it into the bottom of her purse.

No distractions.

Chapter Fifteen

STEPHANIE WAS in her element when it came to being back at work. When she was running lines, acting on set or even in wardrobe, she was at her best. What was totally out of her wheelhouse was attempting to sing for the *Bombshell* soundtrack. Lewis had lined up voice coaches and extra training for Steph, and it had definitely helped, but when she watched Bella in the studio, she was completely in awe. Her friend made it look so easy.

There was a reason Bella was going to be a star.

And fortunately, Steph's singing contribution to the soundtrack was very limited, and she wasn't expected to actually sing at the showcase. A small mercy she was grateful for.

She watched Bella from the sound booth for a few minutes, amazed as she always was at her new friend's effortless professionalism. They'd been back in the city and thrown straight into the studio for almost three days. Steph knew Bella was hurting over what had happened with Jeremy and how they'd left things, but she was doing a damn good job at hiding it.

She didn't want to push her friend to talk, and Bella wasn't offering any details, so Steph didn't actually know how Bella and Jeremy had left things. But she knew it wasn't good because no matter how good a job Bella was doing hiding her feelings, she couldn't totally fool Steph.

When the song was over, Steph caught her eye and waved a little good-bye.

Bella still had hours of work left, but she was done for the day and she finally had the afternoon free. It was time to pay a much overdue visit to another friend who hadn't been all that forthcoming with answers about what was going on.

Twenty minutes later, Steph was knocking on the door to Nick Newton's condo downtown. He lived on the top floor in the penthouse suite, with 360-degree views of the city skyline and the mountains in the distance. Everything was stainless steel, and gleaming white marble countertops, leather couches and white rugs.

It was trendy, if not a little sterile with every surface completely clean and no clutter in sight. The perfect bachelor pad. At least it had been the last time Steph had visited.

Things had changed.

Nick answered the door in sweatpants and an inside-out T-shirt that had a suspicious stain down the front. His normally perfectly combed hair stood up wildly on his head and he sported a scruffy beard. If it wasn't for his familiar black-framed glasses, that were admittedly smudged and covered in fingerprints, Steph wasn't sure she would have recognized him at all.

"Steph." He held the door open. "This is a surprise. I didn't know you were coming."

She leaned in to give him a half hug. "I did tell you I was in town and was going to stop by."

"You did?" He pulled his glasses off and scrubbed at his face. "I'll take your word for it. I'm a little forgetful these days. Come in."

Forgetful was an understatement. He looked as if he hadn't

slept in weeks. Possibly months. How long had it been since she'd seen him? Faith and Logan got married at the end of the summer and he'd disappeared with the baby shortly after that.

Steph followed him into the apartment and stopped short.

Gone were the gleaming white surfaces and the pristine bachelor pad she remembered. She didn't want to draw attention to the mess, but also, there was no way she could ignore it completely.

"Nick?" Steph turned in a wide circle before landing on him. "Are you—"

They were interrupted by the cry of a baby. *The* baby.

Nick's face fell and he dropped his head in defeat. "I just got her..."

"Can I?"

His head shot up, his eyes wide beneath his smudged glasses. "Would you?"

Steph couldn't help but laugh. She wasn't one of those women who instinctively loved babies, but she also wasn't afraid of them. And her friend definitely looked as though he could use a hand. "Show me her room. She's what...four months old now?" The baby had been about a month old when the woman had showed up at Faith and Logan's wedding and dropped the baby in Nick's arms. Claiming it was *his*.

"Five," Nick said. "And she still doesn't like to sleep much."

Steph smiled supportively. She couldn't even imagine being handed a baby out of the blue, completely unprepared for the responsibility of raising a child. From the few phone calls they'd had, she'd assumed Nick was doing okay with it all. He certainly hadn't let on that he was struggling. She felt bad. They didn't know each other well, but she should have tried harder to reach out, because clearly Nick *had* been struggling.

He led the way across his expansive living room. He opened the door to what she assumed was, not long ago, his guest room and was surprised to see a beautiful nursery. A white wooden dresser sat along the far wall. Teddy bears and other various stuffed animals decorated the surface. Across from that was a changing table with piles of diapers and a box of wipes, ready to go. The walls were painted a soft pink, with framed prints of baby animals giving the room a comfortable and very girly feel. On the far wall was the white crib, with a very awake and currently very unhappy baby making it known that she was ready for attention.

Instincts Steph didn't even know she had kicked in as she crossed the room to baby Amelia. It was the first time she'd met the little girl, but Steph was instantly smitten with her.

She bent over the crib and kept her voice low as she tried to calm her. "Ssh, it's okay." Steph reached in and scooped her up. She pressed her gently to her chest and rubbed her back. "It's okay, little one. You just want to say hi, don't you?"

Steph bounced and rocked, and it didn't take long for Amelia to settle. "Well, hello there." She held her away from her a little so she could look at the baby's face. "Aren't you absolutely gorgeous?" And she was. She had a full head of soft, dark hair, a tiny little nose, and Cupid's bow lips. Her blue eyes were electric, and Steph found she could barely look away from the beautiful baby.

"Oh, Nick," she said. "She's perfect."

Nick had collapsed into a rocking chair in the corner of the room. His head fell to his chest and he looked as if he were asleep. She padded across the room and bent a little, the baby still in her arms. She had to swallow her laughter when she saw that Nick *was* fast asleep.

"Why don't we let Daddy sleep for a few minutes?" Steph said to the baby as they slipped from the room. It wasn't until she'd closed the door behind her and gone out to the living room that Steph realized she didn't even know whether Nick *was* the father of baby Amelia.

Steph let Nick sleep for over an hour. When he finally emerged from the nursery, stretching his arms over his head, he looked remarkably better, but there was still room for improvement. Steph sent him to shower and change while she handled things with the baby, who had fallen asleep in her swing. She spent a few minutes tidying up the living room and kitchen, and when Nick rejoined her, finally looking far more like himself, there was a semblance of order to the room.

"Thank you, Steph. Really." Nick joined her on the couch. "I swear, some days I don't even know which way is up. This is all…well, it's a lot."

"I can imagine it is." Steph crossed her legs and examined her friend. "So why are you doing it alone?"

It was the one question she couldn't figure out. Nick was ridiculously wealthy. He and Damon Banks had developed some sort of microchip that had earned them each multiple millions of dollars. He could afford an entire staff to take care of Amelia. Or at least clean up the place.

He shrugged and said simply, "I don't think children should be raised by nannies."

"I don't disagree with that," Steph said carefully. She didn't want to overstep. "But a little bit of help wouldn't be a bad thing, Nick. You know you don't have to do this alone, right?"

He shook his head but didn't meet her eyes. "I really do appreciate you coming by, Steph. I know our relationship didn't really go the way maybe I would have liked…"

He changed the subject so smoothly, Steph caught a glimpse of the Nick she'd met that summer in Glacier Falls. The lighthearted, carefree Nick who had liked to flirt with her. There was more than one person in Glacier Falls who'd thought maybe something would develop between the two of them. And maybe something would have. But he'd taken off so suddenly when Amelia arrived, there hadn't been time to see where it could go.

"Why don't you come spend some time in Glacier Falls? There are lots of people there who'd love to see you and the baby."

He shook his head again. "I don't know. It's all so...well, can I be honest?"

"Please."

"It's embarrassing, Steph. When Lacy showed up like that at the wedding, it was mortifying."

"Lacy? That's Amelia's mother?"

"No." Nick shook his head again. "Lacy is Amelia's aunt. Her mother...well, no one really knows where Jessica is. She kind of dumped the baby on her sister and took off."

"That's terrible."

"Right?" Nick's gaze fell on the sleeping baby and his eyes filled with love. "She doesn't deserve that. To be abandoned by her mother like that. It's not fair."

Steph's heart clenched. Nick had obviously been in so much pain, and he'd been dealing with it alone.

"I hired some investigators to track her down at first. But I called them off."

"What? Why would you do that? You need to find her."

"Do I?" He shrugged. "Jessica didn't want her. Do I really need to bring her back into Amelia's life when she didn't want to be there in the first place? Why? Just so she can leave again?" He shook his head and crossed his arms. "No," he said with resolution. "I won't do that to her."

"So you're punishing yourself because of the sins of her mother? You're not at fault, Nick. You didn't even know you were a father, right?"

Something flashed across his face.

"What?" Steph pressed. "What aren't you telling me?"

He took a deep breath and exhaled slowly. "That's the thing," he said after a moment. "I don't think I am the father."

Amelia chose that moment to wake up. She stretched her little arms over her head and fussed. Still shocked by his revelation, Steph stared, open-mouthed, as Nick jumped up to tend to the baby. Her shock dissolved into impressed warmth as she watched him with the baby. The love he had for Amelia oozed from him.

He cooed and tickled her cheeks until the baby was laughing.

It didn't matter what he'd just revealed to her. Biological father or not, Nick was Amelia's daddy.

She waited another few minutes longer until he had the baby settled into his arm with a bottle.

"Are you going to expand on that little detail?"

He bit his bottom lip and slowly looked up. "I did the math."

Of course he did. That's what Nick did. Math.

"The times don't work out. I dated Jessica, if you can call it that, only for a few weeks. But it was before. If Amelia is mine, it's probably some kind of miracle."

"You haven't done a DNA test?"

She knew the answer.

"I can't." When he looked up into her eyes, there was so much pain on his face. "If I know she's not mine, then…what will happen to her? They'll take her away. Jessica is obviously not fit and Lacy, well, she couldn't get rid of her fast enough. No," he said resolutely. "She's better off with me. No matter what."

Steph let it all settle in. She couldn't disagree with him. Still, there had to be another way. And if he planned to be this baby's father, he was going to need help.

"Enough about all of this," he said before she could take the conversation further. "Tell me what's going on with you.

Did you ever buy that little piece of paradise you were talking about?"

They spent the next few minutes talking about Lynx Creek and her plans. She'd just started telling him about Travis— well, not *all* about Travis. She purposely left out the details on how the man made her want to tear all her clothes off with just a glance and how when he spoke to her, his voice low and sexy, her body reacted and there was a very specific spot between her legs that ached with need. Yes. She left all *those* details out.

Not that it mattered. While they were talking, Steph's phone rang with an incoming video call—as if the man's ears were burning. Her face flushed and Nick laughed.

"Is that your guy now?"

"He's not my guy."

"He's your contractor guy," he said pointedly.

"True. But that doesn't mean he's my guy."

"Sure." Nick nodded. "Either way, I'd say it looks like I have myself some competition."

Steph tipped her head toward the baby in his arms. "I'd say you do, too."

Chapter Sixteen

ALMOST AN ENTIRE WEEK had passed since Jeremy had seen Bella. Or spoken to her.

They'd exchanged a few text messages, but something kept him from picking up the phone and calling her. He knew he should. He *wanted* to. More than anything, he wanted to hear her sweet voice. Well, maybe not as much as he wanted to see her. Touch her. Hold her in his arms. Tell her that he was sorry for being such an asshole, that he never should have suggested in any kind of way that she shouldn't go to the city and follow her dreams.

What had he been thinking?

He hadn't.

No. He *had*.

He'd been thinking of her and him. And their future together. A future that involved them actually in the same city. Once the idea was planted in his head, Jeremy couldn't think of anything else besides being married to Bella. Why shouldn't he have what everyone else had? The happily ever after. The forever.

And kids.

Hope and Levi were about to be parents and soon the others would be, too. And he and Bella...

Shit.

They wouldn't have anything because he was too thick-headed to accept she had dreams and hopes of her own.

"Davis."

Ed Walker's booming voice preceded him as he entered the station lounge.

Jeremy jumped up from the sofa, and the daydream he'd fallen into. "Sir?"

"Next Saturday," Ed announced. "We're going to have a little ceremony for you and me. Good?"

Was he asking or telling? Jeremy couldn't be sure.

"Sounds great," he said.

"Good. The wife is insisting on a retirement thing, and I wanted you to have a formal welcoming. So, we'll just do it all at once. Okay?"

Jeremy couldn't help his smile. "It sounds fantastic. I'll let my family know."

Ed nodded and the smile slipped into a look of concern. "Your sister...she's good?"

Good wasn't the word Jeremy would use. Not yet. But she would be. It would take a little time to undo the damage that Billy had done in only a few months, but she'd get there. *They* would get there. Together.

"She'll be fine, sir. Thank you so much for all your help with that situation. I don't know if I could have done it without you."

Ed put his hand on Jeremy's shoulder. "You would have. Absolutely. But it's always nice to have a little help from time to time. And family is family. I'm glad we could do something for her."

He slapped Jeremy's back, signifying the end of the moment, and said, "Great. So Saturday it is. And maybe see if that girlfriend of yours can sing a little something, too. Her voice…damn. It's something else."

Jeremy swallowed hard. "Sure is, sir. It sure is."

"Maybe something modern," Ed continued. "Or maybe—"

"Well, I don't know if she'll be able to." Jeremy interrupted him before he could get too carried away. "She's pretty busy rehearsing for her new movie. She may have to rest her voice. I'll see what I can do."

He didn't bother telling the other man that he didn't even know whether Bella would be at the ceremony. More than anything, he wanted her for his big moment. To be able to see her sitting in the audience supporting him, and loving him…it would mean so much. *But would she?*

If he asked, would she come? Where had they even left their relationship?

So many questions. And there was only one way to get answers.

Jeremy picked up the phone.

It had been a long week.

But despite Bella's bone-deep exhaustion, she could honestly say that she'd never had so much fun. Rehearsing and performing the songs for the *Bombshell* soundtrack had been amazing. Working with a professional band in a soundstage with real producers…it had been an incredible experience.

"You did awesome."

Bryan, one of her producers, sat across from her at the restaurant. A crew of them had gone out to celebrate the first week of recording. "Steph here," Bryan added, pointing to the superstar, "well, her voice is..."

"Careful," Steph threatened. "Not all of us can have voices like Bella's."

"I was going to say, your voice is second *only* to Bella's."

They all laughed because for all the talents that Steph did have, singing wasn't on the top of her list. She'd done great, that was true. But it had definitely been a lot harder for her.

"I'm just glad my part's over," Steph said. "How are you feeling about the showcase, Bella? It's in a few days already."

Bella groaned. It was coming up quickly. Saturday would be upon them before she knew it. And she'd be ready. She said as much. "It's all happening pretty fast, but I'm excited. The songs are amazing. I can't wait to share them."

"And you'll be sharing them with the world," Bryan reminded her. "This is going to be huge."

"You're ready for this?"

Bella nodded and smiled at Steph's question. "I've been waiting for this for a very long time. I'm ready."

And she was. She'd been dreaming about this since she was a little girl, and everything was finally coming together. The day before, a studio-appointed stylist had visited her with a rack of dresses for her to try on. Each more beautiful than the last. It was like something from a movie as she twirled and spun in front of the mirror while her stylist—*stylist*—had fussed with jewelry and shoe choices. There had been a hair and makeup consult in preparation, and everything was in place for the big day.

Except her date.

More than anything, Bella wanted Jeremy to be there with her. She had dreamed of him walking her down the red carpet, looking dashing in a fitted, black tux. He wouldn't be in the audience, no. But he'd be backstage, where it would feel like he was right there with her. Supporting her.

Not asking her to give up all her dreams and live a small-town life in Glacier Falls.

Not that there was anything wrong with small-town life. Not at all. But it wasn't *her* life. It wasn't her *dream*. And she still couldn't believe he'd stood there and asked her to make a choice.

Well, he hadn't outright asked her. He never got the chance because the chief had called. And the chief always came first. Even if he hadn't been calling about his sister, Charlotte, it wasn't lost on Bella that Jeremy still would have interrupted that important conversation to take that call. He still would have chosen *his* career over her. Yet he was asking her to choose him over her career.

"Stop it."

Steph's voice, followed by a gentle nudge in the ribs, jarred Bella out of her thoughts. She looked at her friend, who was shaking her head.

"Stop thinking about it. You deserve to be here. In this moment. You've earned this, Bella. Soak it all in."

"You're right."

"I know I'm right." Steph laughed. "Besides, we're going to do karaoke."

"Karaoke? Haven't I done enough singing?"

"Oh no," Bryan chimed in. "This isn't *singing*. This is karaoke. You aren't trying unless you're really *not* trying."

Bella couldn't help herself. She laughed. "So, the worse I sing, the better I'm doing?"

"Exactly." Bryan jumped up from the table. "I'll go first. Watch and learn, ladies."

Bella liked Bryan. He was a genuinely nice guy and he really cared about making her experience a positive one. Only a few years older than her, he felt like a brother to her, and he'd made her comfortable almost from the very beginning.

A waitress came by, and Bella ordered another drink as her cell phone rang.

"Put it away!" Steph cried.

"It's probably my mom." Bella laughed as she pulled her phone out from the bottom of her purse. She'd turned it back on a few days after arriving in the city because Lewis almost continually needed to get hold of her. Not that she should have been worried about being distracted by Jeremy. Besides a few very short text messages, he hadn't called.

She flipped her phone over to look at the caller ID.

Until now.

"Oh no." Steph sat up in her seat and reached for Bella's phone. "I know that face, Bella. Don't answer that. Remember, you deserve this. No distractions, right?"

"No distractions." She looked up at Steph apologetically.

There was no way she wasn't answering it.

Resigned, Steph groaned and turned her attention to the stage, where Bryan had started very loudly, and very badly, belting out "Ice, Ice Baby."

Before she could change her mind, Bella pressed the button. "Hello?"

"Bella."

His voice washed through her and sent a warmth to every part of her, like a hug she didn't know she needed. How was it possible that one word from the right person could do that?

"Jeremy." She worked hard to control her voice. Next to her, Bella heard Steph mutter something. She turned her back to her friend. "How are you?"

"I'm sorry I haven't called."

"I haven't called either."

"No."

The word hung between them.

"Bella, I—"

"I hate this—"

They spoke at the same time and it broke the tension between them. "You go first," Bella said with a laugh.

"I miss you."

She exhaled slowly. "I miss you, too."

"Is everything going okay there? You're enjoying it?"

Bella didn't want to read too much into his question. He was only asking because he cared. Not because he was hoping that she hated it and would go running back to Glacier Falls and him. He wasn't like that. She forced the negative feelings away. "I am," she said. "A lot. It's been really busy but so great. I can't remember the last time I sang so much."

"I'm glad you're enjoying it."

Again, Bella couldn't help but think she heard something in his voice. Was that the way it was going to be between them now? She was going to second-guess everything he said and wonder whether he was going to try to get her to come back? Would he ever support her? Did they even stand a chance?

Bella hated herself for doubting him.

"I am. But I'm absolutely exhausted."

"Bella!" Bryan called to her from the stage. "It's your turn next," he half sang into the microphone.

"Who was that?" Jeremy asked. "Are you out somewhere?"

"I actually am." She shook her head no at Bryan, and laughed a little when he pretended to reel her in. "They want me to sing karaoke."

"Sounds fun. I thought you were exhausted?"

She definitely hadn't imagined the inflection in his voice that time.

"I am."

"Are you out with a—"

"Co-worker," she said before he could imply any different. She turned away so she wouldn't be able to see Bryan. "And how are things there?" She shifted the topic to safer subjects. "Has the chief made an official announcement?"

"That's actually why I'm calling. That and of course I miss your voice," he added quickly. "There's going to be a bit of a ceremony to make it all official and welcome me as the chief."

"That's great, Jeremy. You deserve that. This is a big deal."

"It is, isn't it?"

Bella laughed. "Of course it is. Fire chief? That's huge."

"Will you come?"

She couldn't believe he would even have to ask. "Of course. I wouldn't miss it." She sat up straight, a grin on her face despite the fact that he couldn't see it. He'd be able to hear it in her voice and that was important right now. It was *very* important. The divide between them was too wide; she needed to close it however she could. Because yes, she'd been so busy since getting to the city and starting to work, but that didn't mean she hadn't found plenty of time to think about Jeremy and miss him. A lot. "I can't wait to celebrate with you. You absolutely deserve this, Jer. I'm so excited for you."

"Thank you, Bella."

It wasn't her imagination that she heard a sigh of relief in his voice. A softness. Gone was the hesitant, unsure Jeremy he'd been when she'd answered. Happiness filled her. Maybe this was it? Maybe they'd finally be able to get back to each other and fix what was starting to crack between them.

"It means so much that you'll be here, Bella. And I can't wait to see you. Maybe after, on Saturday, we can spend the day together and—"

"Wait." Bella froze. The warmth that had been running through her shifted to a block of ice, and landed in a pit in her stomach. "Saturday? Not this Saturday?" She asked the question, afraid she already knew the answer. "So the ceremony is on Friday?"

"Yes." His answer came slowly. "This weekend. It's fast, but the chief put it all together and his wife kind of went crazy with it and...why?"

"The showcase is on Friday, Jeremy."

"The showcase?"

"You know…with all the stars and—"

"That guy you're out with?"

She shook her head in wonder. "What? You aren't really—"

"No. I…I don't know."

"He's the producer, Jeremy, and yes, it's with everyone. It's a really big deal."

The silence once again hung between them.

"*This* is a big deal, Bella. A really big deal. It's my career. It's the biggest thing in my entire career."

The warmth was gone. They were back to distance.

Bella looked to Steph and Bryan and the others who'd been working so hard on the showcase that was going to launch this massive movie that would absolutely change her life. To say it was a big deal was an understatement. But Jeremy's was a big deal, too.

"I don't know what to say, Jer. This is the biggest thing in my career. I…"

"Will you come?"

She sat back hard in her seat, shocked by his question. "Come? To Glacier Falls?"

"Yes," he said simply. His voice was cold. "Will you come, Bella?"

She shook her head. No. There was no way she could come. The fact that he was even asking her… She looked at Steph, but her friend had joined Bryan on stage to sing. Badly.

No distractions.

Not attending the showcase that was featuring *her* could definitely be considered a distraction. There was no way. And Jeremy knew that. And just like that, he was asking her to choose between him and her dreams. "I'm sorry," she said finally. Her voice was strong. There was no waver, so sure she was in her choice. "If you're making me choose, Jeremy, then I think you know there is no choice to be made."

It wasn't until she disconnected the call that she allowed herself to breathe in. And then before she could let it sink in, she powered off her phone and joined Steph on stage.

No distractions.

Chapter Seventeen

ALMOST AN ENTIRE WEEK had gone by since Jeremy had thrown away everything.

Well, not everything. But he'd thrown away any chance at having Bella.

And that might as well have been everything.

He'd been little more than a zombie for the last few days, going through the motions at the station, responding to minor calls, and putting around between call outs. Nothing mattered. Not without Bella.

Jeremy tried his best to keep his personal heartache away from the fire station and the preparations for the ceremony that would be happening in only a few hours. He didn't want to dampen everyone's joy with his own misery. Especially because the party was also for him.

But he didn't want it.

He'd go through the motions and give his promotion the respect it deserved. But then...what?

"Hey there, brother."

He opened one eye, not bothering to get up from where he lay on the couch in the station lounge.

"Busy working hard, I see. No wonder the chief gave you the promotion." She chuckled and sat down next to him.

It was good to hear Charlotte laugh again. Slowly, since she'd been home, she'd started to come out of her shell a little bit more and more as the threat of Billy on the other side of the country seemed to get further away.

"What are you doing here?"

"The chief needed some childhood photos for the big ceremony tonight. I was happy to bring them down. I mean, any chance to embarrass my little brother… But it looks like you need a hug or something."

"I'm fine."

"I can see that."

"I'm resting."

"You're pouting."

"I'm not pouting."

"I know you."

"I know me better."

"I don't think that's true."

She sounded so self-satisfied, Jeremy took the bait. He pushed himself up to sitting and stared at his sister, whose mouth was set into a smug line.

"Got ya."

He shook his head. As happy as he was to have his sister back in town, and safe, that didn't mean that he was interested in any way in having a deep conversation about his feelings. Or Bella. Or either. She'd made her choice. Never mind that he'd *made* her choose.

Damn. Why had he made her choose?

He scrubbed his hand over his face.

Because he was a moron. That's why.

Only a moron would make his girlfriend choose between the biggest career move of her life and them. Especially when that career move was going to make her a star. He was a selfish prick.

He didn't deserve her.

"You're being an idiot, brother."

"What?" He stared at his sister, instantly defensive despite the fact that she was right. "I'm not—"

The shrill of the siren split the air.

Just as he'd been trained, Jeremy's brain locked in on the alarm and the emergency that was filling the air. He moved automatically while the dispatcher's voice came on.

Fire.

Four alarms.

Big Rock Inn.

That meant people. Potentially lots of them.

Shit.

The hotel looked to be almost completely consumed in flames when they pulled up in front.

How had it gone up so fast?

Jeremy barked orders, his instincts kicking in as everyone jumped into action.

The hoses were secured to the pumper truck.

Jeremy grabbed an ax and along with Natalie by his side, they headed toward the flames.

A crowd had gathered across the street. Residents had responded with blankets and coats for the displaced hotel guests, some of whom were left standing and shivering in the cold, having escaped with nothing.

At least they'd escaped.

He recognized Lori Anderson, the owner of Big Rock Inn, a blanket wrapped around her shoulders as she stood and stared at her hotel burning down. "Is there anyone inside?"

She turned and stared blankly at him before nodding. "I think so. I was able to log in to the registration system from my phone, and I'm not sure if everyone is accounted for, but I think...maybe..."

"What room?"

"Second floor. Room twenty-four."

That was all Jeremy needed to hear.

He was putting his mask on as he moved, single-mindedly, toward the fire. His training kicked in and he moved on autopilot. Going through his checklist.

Tank. Check.

Ax. Check.

Equipment. Check.

He scanned the burning building. Not all of it was consumed by flames. The back staircase would be accessible. If they moved quickly.

Natalie was right behind him.

They got the door down easily, and were greeted by a wall of smoke.

Was that a cry he heard?

Shit.

He moved up the stairs quickly through the thick, black smoke. He'd been in the hotel many times. He knew room twenty-four.

Sure enough, the door was locked when he reached it.

A crash somewhere behind him reminded him that they didn't have much time. The hotel was burning quickly. They only had moments.

He gestured to Natalie, who moved across the hall to check another room while he swung his ax. The door splintered easily and he pushed the debris out of the way as he stepped in.

He could barely see through the smoke, but there, next to the bed. A woman.

He moved toward her, when he heard the cry again.

Frantic, Jeremy spun in the room.

It was a child's cry. *But where?*

He looked to the woman, who was unconscious, and quickly made his decision before moving to the bathroom.

"Stand back," he yelled through his mask. "I need to get the door open."

He heard a muffled response and hoped like hell whoever was on the other side was out of the way as he swung his ax and got the door open.

There, in the bathtub. A child.

Often children got scared in a fire and they'd hide. This little girl may have saved her life by doing that. Still, Jeremy needed to get her and her mother out quickly if any of them stood a chance. He held his hand out, and thankfully she took it. As soon as she was close enough, he scooped her up in his arm and went to her mother. Could he carry them both? He had to try.

The little girl clung to him like a monkey, so he was able to squat and, abandoning his ax, scoop the woman up with his other arm. It wasn't ideal, but he draped her over his shoulder and went to the door.

He could hear Natalie on the radio. She'd found another guest of the hotel and was escorting them out.

He'd have no help.

It didn't matter.

The little girl shifted on his arm in an effort to get to her mother. Jeremy tripped.

Shit.

He couldn't carry them both. It would be faster to do one at a time. It wasn't ideal, but he could do it. He'd have to move fast.

Once the decision was made, Jeremy moved quickly down the stairs, running as fast as his gear would allow him. The moment he hit the fresh, cold air, he thrust the little girl out of his arms to another firefighter. Theo, maybe. It didn't matter. As long as she was safe.

"Jeremy!"

Someone—he didn't know who—yelled out behind him.

"You can't go back in there. Wait for the—"

A second later, he was back inside. The smoke was thicker. It was harder to breathe. Harder to see. But it didn't matter. Adrenaline pumped through him, fueling him and pushing him back up the stairs. He moved on instinct, letting his memory guide him back to the hall outside of room twenty-four where he'd left the woman.

He'd never left anyone behind, and he didn't plan to start today.

Beneath him, a stair gave way under his foot.

Shit. The flames had reached the stairs. He was running out of time.

A renewed push of energy drove him up the stairs where the woman lay.

"Come on," he said to himself. "Time to go."

He scooped her up in his arms and held her as tightly to his chest as he could.

The stairs were almost completely consumed. The flames licked the walls around them. But he couldn't stop. It wasn't an option. They'd both perish. And there was no way that was happening.

Not today. Not like this.

He made it down the stairs and there was a crash behind him. The crackling of the wooden hotel burning up around him grew louder in his ears. *It was hot. So hot.* He was running out of time.

Jeremy moved by memory and instinct alone, hoping desperately that the door to the outside would be right—

Something—falling debris—hit him in the back and flung

him forward toward the door and the fresh air that would save them. Pain seared in back. His head. The woman tumbled from his arms. But the last thought he had before he lost consciousness was of another woman.

Bella.

Chapter Eighteen

IT WAS FINALLY HERE.

The showcase was only hours away and it still didn't feel real to Bella. Nothing felt real.

It had been a long week. A really long week.

Between the intense rehearsals and time in the recording studio, along with all the interviews and press commitments, Bella barely had time to think about how she'd left things with Jeremy. How had it gone so wrong, so quickly when it had all been so very right? It didn't make sense.

And her nighttime hours were filled with trying to make sense of it all. Not that she could. Instead, she tossed and turned; when she could finally fall asleep, her dreams were of Jeremy and everything that could be between them. Until it finally was easier not to sleep at all.

Finally, desperate for some rest, the night before the showcase, she gave in and took a sleeping pill.

She woke up the next morning, ready and rested. She'd also woken up to dozens of unread messages and missed calls on her phone.

She probably should have looked at them. But the idea of

reading messages from loved ones wishing her well on her big day but not seeing a message from Jeremy was too much. She couldn't handle it, so she powered off her phone and tucked it into a drawer.

Today was the biggest day of her career. She needed to focus.

Besides, she had come to the conclusion that it wasn't the right time to have a relationship. It was for the best that they weren't together. Logically, she knew that.

But logically or not, it didn't matter. Because when she closed her eyes, she could still see him. She could feel his touch. Taste his kiss.

All of it.

It was too much.

Even if it was *for the best*. She still wasn't capable of reading a message from him and knowing he wouldn't be in the audience watching her, supporting her and loving her. And likewise, she wouldn't be there for him on his big day.

Every time she thought of it and all they were both missing, there was a physical pain in her chest. The weight of it all was crushing.

It was easier not to think of it at all.

She went through the motions of eating her breakfast, an egg-white omelette her nutritionist had ordered up for her. She'd been staying in a suite on the second-top floor of the hotel near the studio instead of her own small apartment. It was more convenient to be close to everything and because the studio was paying for it, and there was a chef to make all her food that the nutritionist had laid out for her, it was all just easier. Steph had the top floor, the penthouse suite. Bella may be the star of the movie, but Steph was *the* star. Bella was nowhere near at her level of fame. And probably never would be. Even if *Bombshell* was the hit everyone thought it would be, she still wouldn't be at Steph's level.

Even if she wanted to.

And did she?

If it meant not being with Jeremy, ever?

Is that what she wanted?

Sometimes it felt as if she didn't know what she wanted anymore.

She sighed and forced it all from her mind. She needed to focus on the showcase today. That was it. Nothing else.

Bella still had a quick sound check and then she'd be in the makeup and hairstylist chair for a few hours before show time. Oh, and also the red carpet.

Her first red carpet.

And she'd walk it alone.

When Jeremy finally opened his eyes, he was in the hospital. His chest ached. It was hard to breathe and his head pounded.

But he was alive.

He didn't remember anything after running into the burning building for the second time. It had been hot and dark. The smoke.

The woman.

His eyes flew open, and instantly he snapped them shut again against the blinding light of the hospital.

"You're awake."

"Oh, thank goodness."

He recognized his mother and his sister.

But the woman…

He forced himself to open his eyes again and tried to sit up in his bed. "Is she…" He attempted to speak but had to clear his throat. "Is she okay?" he finally asked. "The woman? Did I—"

"She's fine." Jeremy's mother took his hand and squeezed.

"You saved her. She's going to be fine." A tear slipped down her cheek. It looked like it had been one of many.

"And you're going to be fine, too." Charlotte took his other hand. "But holy shit, little brother, you can't scare me like that again. I don't know if I can handle it."

"You both can handle it." His father loomed over him. His smile was cautious, but when he saw Jeremy's face, it split wide. "Damn, son. You really gave us all a fright."

"What happened?"

"The hotel went up fast. Something about some old wires," Dwayne started. "You were hit in the back by some falling debris right before you made it out. Thankfully, the force knocked you forward and the others were able to drag you out. But your back might be—"

"Oh, that explains why I feel like I've been run over by a truck." He tried to shift in the bed, but his whole body ached, and a flash of pain spiked in his head.

"I'll get the doctor," Char said. "You might need some pain meds."

"I don't think there's any question about that."

He tried to smile, but then a fresh thought hit him. The thoughts that had occupied his dreams while he'd been unconscious. "Bella."

His parents exchanged a glance. "She's not—"

"She's okay, right? She's not…" He didn't really know what he was trying to ask. Logically, Jeremy knew it wasn't Bella in the fire who he was trying to save. But he couldn't seem to separate the thought of her and the woman he'd rescued moments before being knocked out. She'd dominated his dreams and it felt so real. "Is she here?"

Darlene shook her head. "No."

"What day is it?"

"It's still Friday," Dwayne said. "The chief said he'd postpone—"

"The showcase is today." Jeremy struggled to a seated position. "It's Bella's big day. I need to go."

"You need to rest." His mother's hand was on his chest. "The doctor will be in, and you—"

"No. You don't understand." He wasn't sure he understood either. At least not fully. But while he'd been asleep, there'd been something. *Someone.* Bella.

He needed to try to make sense of it all. And there was only one way to do that.

Bella.

"I have to go." He ignored the pain in his back and his head, and pushed himself up so he was sitting. The world swayed a little, but he forced himself to focus. "I need to get to Bella."

"You aren't going anywhere, son. You need to rest. The doctor will—"

"Keep me here. And I can't...I need to—"

"You need to rest." The doctor appeared, Charlotte right behind him in the doorway. She gave him an apologetic glance, but Jeremy didn't have time for it. "You took quite a hit to the back of your head, Jeremy, and I can't release you until I—"

"I'd like to release myself."

"No!"

His mother clung to him, but Jeremy forced himself to look squarely at the doctor. He knew his body. He was fine. He'd taken a hit before. He'd be sore and have some aches and pains to be sure, but he'd recover. Physically. However, that wouldn't be the case if he didn't get to Bella and make sure she understood how much he loved her and would choose her over and over again no matter what.

That's what was clear.

That's what came to him while he'd been unconscious. It was all Bella. It was always all Bella.

Nothing mattered without her.

Not the fire chief position. Not living in Glacier Falls.
Not...living.

Nothing.

It had been a full day and Bella had been successful with
complete focus on the showcase.

Mostly.

Her thoughts had swayed a few times as she imagined
Jeremy getting ready to accept his promotion. He'd look so
handsome in his dress uniform. So proud. So strong.

Bella blinked and looked back to the mirror and her own
reflection. She hardly recognized herself. Her long, dark hair
had been styled into shiny black waves that fell elegantly down
her bare back. The dress they'd finally settled on was an ivory,
almost silver satin that both hugged her curves and draped
elegantly.

She looked like a goddess and had never before felt so
glamourous. She felt like a bombshell. And she was ready.

Bella took another minute to look at herself in the
mirror.

She'd already walked the red carpet. It was a lot different
than she'd imagined and almost surreal as cameras flashed all
around her. She'd posed and smiled and walked just the way
she'd been coached. There'd been no questions. Those would
come later. After the showcase. So after her brief walk, she was
back in her changing room for a few minutes of silence and
calm before she hit the stage.

A sharp knock on the door, followed by Steph bursting into
her dressing room, startled her.

"Bella. I need to...oh, wow. You look...wow."

"I could say the same." She turned and grabbed her
friend's hands. They'd put Steph in a black, sequined gown.

The contrast of her red hair against the dark, shimmery fabric was startlingly gorgeous.

But Steph wasn't smiling. Her lips, painted a bold red to contrast with her dress, were set into a frown.

"What's wrong?"

"Have you heard from anyone today?"

Bella shook her head. Her phone was still safely in her dresser drawer in her hotel room. *No distractions.* But something in her friend's face told her that maybe she should have had her phone.

"What's going on?"

"Five minutes, ladies." Bryan popped his head into the dressing room. "You both look stunning. Ready to go?"

Steph nodded and gave him a sweet smile. "Just give us one minute, Bryan?"

A flicker of worry crossed his face, but he nodded. "But just one. I need you both on set."

"Don't worry, Bryan. We'll be there." Steph's voice was calm and soothing. Rehearsed.

Bella almost forgot the look that had been on her friend's face a moment earlier. A look that had been anything but calm and soothing.

As soon as Bryan left, Stephanie turned around and took Bella by the hands. "I wasn't sure if I should tell you this or not. But then…well, I know I'd want to know."

Her heart had already stopped and once again stuttered to life at Stephanie's first words. Something was wrong. *Very* wrong.

"What is it?"

"You really haven't heard from anyone?"

She shook her head. "My phone is back in my room. I left it there this morning. You said no distractions."

"Right." Steph nodded. "And that's probably a—"

"Tell me. Now."

"We have to go on in a few minutes."

"I will."

"I'm so sorry to tell you this, Bella. But it's Jeremy. There's been a fire."

Everything stopped. Time froze.

Jeremy.

Fire.

All she could see was his face. Larger than life. He was there in front of her. And then, just as if someone pushed the button to start the video again, everything came to life in vivid color. The floor tilted beneath her, and Steph had to reach out to support her.

"Are you—"

"Jeremy." She brushed off whatever Steph had been about to ask. Nothing else mattered. "Is he...is he okay?"

"I've sent a—"

"Ladies! You need to get on stage."

"What?" Bella ignored Bryan and turned to Steph. "What did you—"

"Two minutes!" Bryan bellowed from the hallway. "Ladies. I need you out here *now*."

Bella looked at Steph in panic. "I can't. I..."

"You can and you will. Jeremy is...he's fine. He's going to be okay. He's in the hospital now and... He wouldn't want you to not do this, Bella. Not because of him."

Her head spun.

Jeremy. Fire. Showcase. Hospital.

He'd asked her not to. He'd asked her to choose. And she'd chosen this. And now... But that was before...that was before the fire. *What if he wasn't okay? What if she lost him? If he asked her again...*

Bella shook her head. "No."

Steph moved so she stood directly in front of her. She was petite, but she made up for it in presence. She grasped Bella by the shoulders and stared her in the eyes. "You know in your heart that no matter what he said when he was hurting, he wants this for you. More than anything, he does. Because he loves you. Do this for him, Bella."

How could she be expected to go on? She couldn't. She needed to...

"It's go time, Bella." Bryan's hand was on her back, urging her forward. "You've got this. You're going to be great."

"Do it for Jeremy, Bella."

Jeremy.

She'd do anything for him.

She nodded numbly, took a deep breath, and, with all eyes on her, put a smile on her face just the way she'd rehearsed and stepped out onto stage.

———

She didn't know how she did it. But somehow, the music took hold and when Bella opened her mouth, the words came out. She closed her eyes and saw Jeremy's face while she sang. She felt him there with her.

One song after the next, each one sounded better than the last. She sang her heart out for almost two hours and completely lost herself in the music.

There was a small audience made up mostly of media and industry people. Bella's parents and grandfather were there, but she didn't allow herself to look down. She couldn't. If she saw the empty chair that Jeremy should have been in...

It didn't matter that he hadn't planned to be there...that he should have been at his own ceremony. He should be receiving his own accolades right now. But he was lying in a hospital and...

Tears filled her eyes and she heard her voice crack a little.

It was the finale. A powerful song of love lost.

Bella could only hope the audience would think her

emotion was because of the song she was performing and not her own love lost. *Almost* lost.

Jeremy was okay. He was in the hospital. She could have lost him. But she didn't. And she wouldn't.

She'd go to him. She'd make it right. She'd...

Her voice faltered as a sob rose up in her chest. She dropped her head, unable to continue.

Jeremy.

The music continued around her as the orchestra played on.

"Bella."

It was her imagination. It had to be. But it sounded just like Jeremy. His voice in her ear. His voice urging her on. *But...*

Her eyes flew open and she lifted her head to finally look at the audience.

And Jeremy.

In the front row. Dressed in scrubs and sitting in a wheelchair, but it was him.

But how?

Bella turned, searching for Steph backstage. Her friend stood in the wings with a smile on her face. She gestured to Bella to keep going. "No distractions." She mouthed the words and then shook her head, but Bella got the meaning.

She turned and without missing another beat, continued singing.

This time, with Jeremy there and okay, there was a renewed energy in her singing. She belted out the finale and as the final notes played, Bella locked eyes with Jeremy. With everything she had, she hoped he could read all of the emotions in her eyes. All the love she had for him. And that she'd never again walk away from it.

Chapter Nineteen

SEEING BELLA ON STAGE, looking every bit the movie star she was about to be, was a moment Jeremy would never forget. She looked like an angel, and her voice…it filled him. Being there, hearing her, he knew in that moment he couldn't have been anywhere else.

And the fact that he'd asked her not to do it killed him. The memory of that moment caused him physical pain that was far beyond what he'd felt when he woke in the hospital.

When she sang the last note, looking straight at him, into his soul, he knew that no matter what had happened between them, it would be okay. They were meant to be together. He knew that with the same certainty that he needed air to breathe. She was his. He was hers. Always.

He sat, transfixed, eyes only for her as the crowd roared to life around him. It wasn't until the curtains closed and the lights came up in the auditorium that Jeremy blinked.

Next to him, Charlotte, who'd accompanied him, and the nurse they'd insisted upon as a condition of release from the hospital, both wiped their eyes.

"Mr. Davis?" A man with a headset appeared. "My name is

Bryan." He walked around to the back of his wheelchair. "You're needed backstage."

Without waiting for a response, the man clicked off the brakes of the chair the nurse had insisted on and moved him quickly up a ramp into the dark curtained backstage area where Bella stood.

"Jeremy." She ran to him, but stopped short before throwing herself into his arms. She looked at him, her hands fluttering in front of her.

"I'm okay. I won't break."

It was all she needed to hear. Bella threw herself into his arms and onto his lap. He held her tight to him as his mouth found hers.

"I'm just so...when I heard...Jeremy..." She pressed her head into his shoulder and began to sob. It was all Jeremy could do not to cry along with her. The emotions of the last... well, too long...threatened to overflow. He held her, the feel of her giving him strength. He breathed deep, the scent of her filling him, giving him the energy he needed.

She was all he needed.

She was all he would ever need.

"Bella," he murmured. "I was wrong," he said. "I was so wrong."

She lifted her head enough to look at him. Mascara streaked down her beautifully made-up face, but she'd never looked so gorgeous.

"I was wrong," he said again. It was important. She needed to hear him. *Really* hear him. "Nothing matters more than you. Not Glacier Falls. Not the fire chief job. Nothing. All I could think of in that hospital was you and that I'd never hear your voice again and never see your face." He reached up and wiped a tear from her cheek. "Nothing matters but you. I was so wrong to ask you—"

"No." She stopped him. "It was me. I...the thought of not

having you…there's just no point to any of this without you, Jer." She cupped his face in her hands. "I need you. I don't want any of this without you."

"I don't want anything without you."

They stared at each other for a few minutes before she started to laugh. He joined in for a moment, but it hurt his ribs and his back.

"Well," Jeremy said. "What are we going to do then, babe? Because I am never letting go of you again."

The laughter died on her lips and she looked at him very seriously. "There's only one thing to do."

He nodded, because it had always been the only option in front of them.

She leaned close and whispered against his lips. "You and me, babe. We're going to have it all."

She meant exactly what she'd said. And she also knew it was possible.

They *could* have it all. And they would.

Because there was no other option. They'd tried it and hell, it had almost killed Jeremy.

Not that them being apart had anything to do with the accident, but Bella chose to believe in fate. And there was no point in tempting it. Not when it came to the two of them. They were meant to be together and that's exactly where they were going to be.

Together.

As much as possible. Because shooting a movie wasn't forever. It's not as if she would have to move permanently. And if she did, well, they'd figure that out then.

In the meantime, she was sure they could make it work.

When there was love, there was always a way.

They kissed more, Bella melting into his arms. She would have happily stayed just like that, on his lap, for the rest of the night. Because as far as she was concerned, it was the perfect way to end a special day.

She was so consumed with Jeremy, Bella hadn't noticed her parents and Papa, waiting to offer their congratulations as well. Not until Papa cleared his throat loudly.

She lifted her head and smiled when she saw him. "You made it."

Bella gave Jeremy another look, almost to make sure he wouldn't disappear if she left him for another moment and went to embrace her family.

"You were amazing, kiddo." Her dad, visibly choked up, squeezed her hard and kissed her on the cheek.

Her mother embraced her and looked over her shoulder to Jeremy. "And the two of you…"

Bella nodded to her unasked question. "We're going to be okay."

Lisa nodded and smiled.

"What about your old Papa? Come here and give me a hug, baby girl. You were…I'm just so…" Roy's rough exterior gave way to his emotion and tears streamed down his face as Bella hugged him. "I've never been so proud in my whole life, Bella. You were born for this."

His voice shook and Bella couldn't speak for fear of crying herself. Even more than she already had.

"Thank you all, for…" Bella stepped back to look at her family. She took Jeremy's hand in hers. "It means so much to have you all here." She looked at Jeremy in his wheelchair. "So much," she said, her voice breaking.

"Bella?" Behind her, Bryan cleared his throat. "I tried to give you some time, but…" She turned and he visibly jumped back. "Oh wow." He reached for the button on his radio. "We're going to need makeup for Ms. Burton."

Did she look that bad? Bella laughed. Probably.

"You're gorgeous," Jeremy said, reading her mind. "But he's right. You probably still have things to do."

She tilted her head. She couldn't leave him. He was just out of the hospital. She took in his scrubs, the hospital bracelet still on his wrist, and raised her eye in question.

"I'll tell you later," he said before, gently and reluctantly, giving her a nudge. "Go. Do what you need to. And I'll be right here." He looked over her shoulder. "Or wherever Bryan tells me to be."

"I'll sort you out, buddy. Don't worry."

Bella smiled between them and nodded. She gave Jeremy a quick kiss on the nose. "Okay. But don't go far."

"I'll take good care of him," Bryan said.

Before she could respond again, she was swooped up by the hair and makeup staff, who went to work on her like a well-oiled machine. Next to her, Michael, her publicist, started running through what was about to happen.

She'd completely forgotten about the question-and-answer period with the cast. She forced herself to listen as he repeated all the things he'd been telling her for the last few days about how to answer the questions. What to say, what not to say.

"And when it comes to…the man…" Michael stuttered over his words. "How would you like to…"

That was an easy one. Bella smiled and looked straight ahead. "He's my fiancé."

Next to her, she heard him take in a gasp of air. No doubt Michael hadn't been briefed on it. Especially considering it wasn't really official. But there was no time like the present and really, what more would it take? When you knew, you knew.

And she knew.

There was no one Bella would rather spend her life with.

And that's exactly how she answered the question fifteen minutes later as she sat on the set with Stephanie Starz, and

Scott Hillman and Rory Marks, the two leading men of the film.

She looked to Steph, who smiled supportively. Bella didn't know how she'd gotten him there so fast—it must have taken a miracle—but she also knew that if anyone could pull it off, Steph could. Getting Jeremy there was all her doing, and she'd never been more thankful for her new friend. Stephanie winked and quickly turned to answer her own question about her personal life.

Bella soaked it all in. After all, the showcase was just the beginning.

And now, she not only had *Bombshell*, she had the love of her life as well. He was safe. He was hers. And that was all that mattered.

They'd figure out the rest later.

Because they had time.

They had forever.

Chapter Twenty

TAKING care of Jeremy was the least Stephanie could do.

Even then, it hardly seemed like enough.

It wasn't Stephanie's fault that there'd been a fire. And it hadn't even been her fault that Jeremy and Bella had broken up. But maybe it kind of was. After all, she'd more or less told Bella that relationships were impossible when you lived in the limelight. She was supposed to be Bella's mentor, and she'd led her away from the thing—or in this case—the person who was exactly right for her.

Logan called to let her know that Jeremy was in the hospital but he was fine. Or would be. He had a minor concussion and the doctor refused to release him without the care of a nurse. Stephanie had done what anyone would do.

Well, anyone with an unlimited bank account and resources at her fingertips.

She'd had her assistant organize a nurse and a helicopter, and had Jeremy flown in for the showcase. It was pretty incredible how fast you could make things happen when you threw money at it. He'd arrived a little over halfway through the showcase, but Bella hadn't noticed. Not until it mattered.

And now, watching their reunion, Steph knew that it really was all that mattered. The love between them was everything.

"That was a pretty nice thing you did." Nick, along with baby Amelia, equipped with headphones to protect her ears, joined her. "Also, you look stunning."

He gave her a kiss on the cheek. There were no fireworks with Nick, but there was a comfort. Being with him was easy and nice.

Maybe that was love?

She looked at her friend. He was handsome and dependable and successful in his own right. And she loved him. But… it wasn't the same thing.

"I'm glad you could make it," she said, ignoring his compliments. "It means a lot to have you here." Faith, Hope, Logan, and Levi would have been there as well, but with the short notice…Faith and Logan had a wedding at the ranch, and Hope really shouldn't be traveling. So they'd decided to stay put. It was nice to have Nick there to support her. And of course baby Amelia, who Steph was becoming more and more smitten with every time she saw her.

"And you look so pretty tonight, too, kiddo."

The baby cooed with the attention.

The question period was done and there was nothing left but the after party, which thankfully they'd decided to keep simple with cocktails in the lobby of the auditorium for the cast and invited guests.

Stephanie felt wrung out. She wasn't sure she could keep up the act of the gracious actress all night when all she really wanted to do was go back to her hotel room, put on some sweatpants, and curl up with a good book.

"It really is nice to have you here," she said to Nick. "And you also look very handsome."

He straightened his shoulders and gave her a wink. "I do know how to rock a suit, don't I?"

She laughed. "You do. Even with that little spot of spit-up on the shoulder."

"No." He twisted and tugged at his jacket before shrugging and laughing along with her. "It is what it is, and it's all part of this."

"It's a look that suits you, Nick," she said honestly.

It was a hard situation, but being adopted herself, Stephanie could appreciate the value in being raised by good parents. She wouldn't trade hers for anything in the world. Maybe Nick wasn't Amelia's father, but he'd be a damn good dad. And if he wanted to take that on, well...she would fully support her friend.

"I've been thinking a lot about what you said, Steph. About going back to Glacier Falls."

"Oh yeah?"

"It would be good to have some support around." Nick shifted Amelia in his arms. "I think I was just so...well, I was and am still overwhelmed, but I was also afraid of what everyone would think. And then...I mean, she's not...well...it's just a lot and I don't think I was ready to bring all of that into a new group of friends I don't really know and—"

"I get it." She put her hand on his arm. "I do."

He nodded. "I know you do." Nick gestured to where Bella, Jeremy, and the woman she assumed was Jeremy's sister were sitting.

Steph had seen the nurse in the lobby with a plate of appetizers and a glass of champagne earlier, but she wouldn't tell. Jeremy seemed to be doing just fine. Better than fine, with Bella's hand in his.

"What you did for them today," Nick said.

"It was nothing. Anyone would have done it."

"That's just it," Nick said. "Anyone in Glacier Falls would have done it."

She tilted her head in question.

"See," Nick said. "I've noticed that it's not just you with a huge heart. It's Damon, and Katie and the Turner sisters and…well, an entire town of big hearts that would do anything for the people they care about, and that's what I want for Amelia. I want her to be surrounded by people like that. So I've decided that maybe it's time I go back and spend some time with Amelia there."

Steph threw her arms around both Nick and the baby. "I think that's a fabulous idea. You're going to love what I'm doing with Lynx Creek. And maybe you can even give me some ideas for the place? It will be so good to have you back. Come on." She released him from her hug and grabbed his free hand. "I can't wait to tell Bella and Jeremy."

Steph did a quick introduction for Bella, who hadn't officially met Nick yet, and they were all introduced to Charlotte, Jeremy's sister. Steph knew there was a story as to how she'd come back to Glacier Falls, but the very little she did know was that it wasn't a good time to ask for details.

Charlotte took an immediate liking to baby Amelia and had scooped her away from Nick, who sat by, watching closely with a smile on his face.

Bella and Jeremy could hardly keep their hands off each other, and were doing a very poor job pretending that they were even trying, which made Steph laugh. Just being surrounded by her friends filled her with love.

Her parents had video-called earlier and sent their love as they were unable to be there.

The only thing missing were her sisters, and she knew they wouldn't have missed it if there was another option. And they'd all be there for the premiere, and with a new little niece or nephew. The thought made her smile.

Nick's phone rang. He made a quick apology as he glanced at the number and frowned. "Hello?"

Steph leaned over to tickle the baby's toes and give him

privacy in his call, but a moment later, Nick handed her the phone. "It's for you. It's Faith."

"Faith?"

"She said she tried everyone and then remembered that you'd mentioned I was coming tonight, so…" He shook the phone at her.

Stunned, she was still staring at it.

"Right." Steph grabbed it. "Faith? What are you calling me on—"

"It's the baby." Faith cut her off.

Three words and Steph's life flipped upside down.

"It's too early, Steph." Faith's voice shook. "Hope's in the hospital. They're trying to stop it, but…you need to come. Quickly."

I hope you enjoyed Jeremy and Bella's journey to happiness! But wait! What happened after the showcase? Click here for an exclusive bonus scene and find out what happened later that night!

And coming next, Jeremy's partner, Natalie Collins is new to town and ready to start a new life, but will the memories of her past keep her from opening up to Aiden Adams, the sexy high school teacher with eyes only for her? Find out in Finding Happily Ever After!

About the Author

Elena Aitken is a USA Today Bestselling Author of more than forty romance and women's fiction novels. The mother of 'grown up' twins, Elena now lives with her very own mountain man in the heart of the very mountains she writes about. She can often be found with her toes in the lake and a glass of wine in her hand, dreaming up her next book and working on her own happily ever after.

To learn more about Elena:
www.elenaaitken.com
elena@elenaaitken.com